John Rogers Rees

The Brotherhood of Letters

John Rogers Rees

The Brotherhood of Letters

ISBN/EAN: 9783337384142

Printed in Europe, USA, Canada, Australia, Japan

Cover: Foto ©Andreas Hilbeck / pixelio.de

More available books at **www.hansebooks.com**

THE BROTHERHOOD

OF

LETTERS.

BY

J. ROGERS REES,

AUTHOR OF

"THE DIVERSIONS OF A BOOKWORM," "THE PLEASURES OF A
BOOKWORM," ETC.

> " *Ah, did you once see Shelley plain,*
> *And did he stop and speak to you ?*
> *And did you speak to him again ?*
> *How strange it seems, and new !*"
>   ROBERT BROWNING.

NEW YORK :
LOCKWOOD & COOMBES, 275, FIFTH AVENUE.
1889.

CONTENTS.

I.

IMAGINATION DEMANDED OF THE READER.

> "*It is the nature of the soul to appropriate all things. . . . I conquer and incorporate them in my own conscious domain. His virtue,—is not that mine? His wit,—if it cannot be made mine, it is not wit.*"—EMERSON : "Compensation."

> "*My respiration rose; I felt a rapid fire colouring my face. . . . I was Eucharis for Telemachus, and Erminia for Tancred; however, during this perfect transformation, I did not yet think that I myself was anything, for anyone. The whole had no connection with myself; I sought for nothing around me; I was them, I saw only the objects which existed for them; it was a dream, without being awakened.*"—MADAME ROLAND's description of her first reading of Telemachus and Tasso.

THE gods need never trouble themselves to bestow a greater gift upon a favourite child than a powerful and healthy imagination. I use the word "healthy" as a qualifier, knowing right well, with every student of literary biography, that an untamed imagination, running riot and causing its possessor to indulge in all kinds of freaks, mental and otherwise, is often a curse. Let there, however, but be mixed with it in its original bestowment a spice of pure and honest reasonableness—a wee grain of the power to look at everyday facts as they are—and the future of the chosen child of the gods is assured.* *Without* this "wee grain" on board ship the unmanaged sails will prove but playthings for wildest winds, and the craft be thrown on all kinds of perilous rocks; but *with* it its course will be pursued with ease and harmony; still rapid, but safe.

---

* One is tempted to parody the axiom of the elder Shandy, and to say: "An ounce of judgment, in its proper place, is worth a ton of fancy, running wild."

To read literary biography rightly and with fullest enjoyment, a man should certainly possess this healthy imagination. Were I a phrase-coiner, I would say that in his case it should attain its fullest development as an inquisitive-realistic-imagination; and for fear of being thought a heaper-up of unnecessary words, I will go a little further with these words of mine, which threaten to hang about in plenty just here. A writer of biography occasionally works as an artist; he has carefully gone through the materials at hand and formed for himself the picture he desires his readers to see. This he generally gives, and no one can blame him ; for his natural bias has been (we will suppose) honestly followed, and his best is the result. Not so, however, always. Another writer of biography or autobiography will run in the cart-rut he finds in front of him ; he has no theory, no

ideal ; he goes along with the simple
intent to get to the end, spreading
out as he goes all his available
facts; and when he has finished
he mentally says to his readers :
" There, you have all that can
be known of the subject." Well
and good ; we find no fault with
such a recorder. Every fact is valuable in the life of a great man, as
Boswell no doubt thought, and as
Rousseau certainly did think. But
as the feast-giver does not consider
his own tastes only, so the writer is
not the only interested party; his
readers come in for consideration.
One says as he cons the production :
" This incident I like. It is just
what should have been related of
such a man ; it throws floods of
light in upon his personality. Admirable work !" But another turns
up his nose, and exclaims : " What
humbug to be sure ! The subject of

this book was a hero; why should I have thrust upon my notice particulars of where he walked with his wife, and what he said to his gardener?" Here, then, lies the trouble; we as writers go wrong with some classes of readers, and we as readers run afoul of certain biographers. And painters and art-critics with *their* " schools " tread the same thorny path. Yet, after all, what a miserable world this would be but for these differences, and these wise veilings by Providence of the pure and central truth ! for

" Absolute truth revealed, would serve to blind
　The soul's bright eye, and sear with tongues of
　　flame
　The sinews of the mind."

Each individual's predilections make his light *the* light, his truth *the* truth.

Bearing in mind, then, these variations of human taste and judgment, we see how valuable a gift to a reader, especially of biography, is the inquisitive-realistic-imagination to which we have referred.   Inquisitive the reader must be, otherwise he will be satisfied with any writer's estimate of a great man.   But he rather wishes to know all the kinds of opinions shared by the hero of his mood ; no incident is too trifling for him to feel an interest in it; no conversation too vapid if but the man took a part therein. Realistic he must needs also be ; for after he has discovered all about his hero he involuntarily commences the sifting process, and fastens on to certain occurrences or words to be dwelt upon at length with a more fervent interest than others : his realism pounces upon what his subject said or did on matters which have an especial interest for him, and which are peculiarly suited to his considerations ; and, like the bee upon the flower, having settled upon it, he occupies his position till all the honey he cares for has been extracted. I should, perhaps, rather say that his realism focusses his powers of attention upon the attractive spot ; and then, like the tiny portion of rock covered by the limpet, it is for the nonce his world to the entire exclusion of all else. His fast-sticking realization of the matter, narrowing though it prove for the time, is powerful and effective; and above all things it serves his purpose. But it is his imagination which breathes the breath of life upon what of the fruits of his inquisitiveness his realism has settled upon and made its own ; and then, lo ! the thing lives, and is (to him at all events) supremely satisfying.

This threefold gift, then—inquisitive-realistic-imagination—has in it the elements of happiness ; breadth certainly should be its concomitant.

It enables a reader to pick definitely and decidedly for himself out of varied stores ; and it seals the choice by clothing what has been selected in garments which for him have symmetry, and in colours which to his eyes are beautiful.

> " You say you're fair, you know ;
> 'Tis our fancy makes you so."

The following pages are written for those who find enjoyment in musing and brooding, and repeating their lives through memory.* Imagination is certainly necessary to any enjoyment of them. " Truth is one and poor, like the cruse of Elijah's widow. Imagination is the bold face that multiplies its oil."

And it is possible for a man of imagination to make a very heaven

---

* " Come, I will tell you a way how you may live your time over again. Do but recollect, and review what you have seen already, and the work is done."—*Marcus Aurelius.*

for himself out of very trifling elements. His fancy, warmed by a
sensitive and passionate heart, can
clothe the most everyday occurrences
with a golden garb.* Realities may
be coarse, and in some cases ugly
and heavy and oppressive, and there
may be little that is truly sweet and
beautiful in many lives. But we
have our dreams! "We are ill at
ease whilst we remain glued to earth,
hobbling along on our two feet which
drag us wretchedly here and there in
the place which impounds us. We

---

* In a recent after-dinner speech, Mr. George
Augustus Sala, in replying for Literature, said he
once knew a very worthy old citizen of Edinburgh
who settled his quarterly accounts with unfailing
punctuality, but always deducted 15 per cent., on
the ground that he had been intimate with Sir
Walter Scott. Continuing, Mr. Sala confessed
that his own claim to return thanks for Literature
was that he had been on intimate terms with, indeed the disciple and, after a manner, the pupil
of two great men of letters of the last generation—Charles Dickens and William Makepeace
Thackeray. It was simply through his connection
with those giants of literature that he had the
honour to respond to the toast.

need to live in another world, to hover in the wide-air kingdom, to build palaces in the clouds, to see them rise and crumble, to follow in a hazy distance the whims of their moving architecture and the turns of their golden volutes.   In this fantastic world, again, all must be pleasant and beautiful, the heart and senses must enjoy it, objects must be smiling or picturesque, sentiments delicate or lofty ; no crudity, incongruity, brutality, savageness, must come to sully with its excess the modulated harmony of this ideal perfection."*   In a life of dreams spent among the notable literary men of the past, we claim that it is possible to know an enjoyment neither coarse nor vulgar, but eminently restful, and conducive to mental health.

It appears to us that Alfred Austin succeeded in laying his hand on the

* Taine.

hem of Truth's garment when he declared that "whatever the beloved Children of the Muse may fondly think, the world cares very little for poetry, however much interest it may show in certain poets.* It is, nevertheless, interested in poets the incidents of whose lives resemble those of a first-rate novel, or whose biography can be made to resemble a prose romance."†

And what poetry can equal that of a possible life? "If, invisible ourselves, we could follow a single human being through a single day of his life, and know all his secret thoughts and

* A pretentious lady once said, at a notable gathering, that she had "never read Shakespeare's works herself, but had always entertained the *highest opinion of him as a man.*"

† The Autocrat of the Breakfast-Table in *one* of his many moods says: "I know the man I would have—a quick-witted, out-spoken, incisive fellow . . . who cares for nobody, except for the virtue there is in what he says ; delights in taking off big wigs and professional gowns, and in the disembalming and unbandaging of all literary mummies."

hopes and anxieties, his prayers and tears and good resolves, his passionate delights and struggles against temptation—all that excites and all that soothes the heart of man—we should have poetry enough to fill a volume. Nay, set the imagination free, like another bottle-imp, and bid it lift for you the roofs of the city, street by street, and after a single night's observation you may sit down and write poetry and romance for the rest of your life."* The merest incident tinged with unusual colour, or exhibiting other than ordinary fulfilment, is sufficient to furnish an excellent foundation; and the castle built thereon towers into the clouds which hide exalted regions from the gaze of the multitude. And what a life we live in it ! All that is prosaic and commonplace is lost in the shadowy distance. Ours is the life

* Longfellow.

on the hill, and we see not the valley below, where the patient bondman toils like a beast of burden : we associate with heroes, nay, with gods— and of our own making. We see the tree-tops waving in the wind, and hear the merry birds singing under their green roofs ; and we choose to forget for the time that at their roots there are swine feeding upon acorns.

Given, for instance—and to cease with figures of speech—the fact that two notable men, with refined tastes in common, spent a certain evening together, discoursing on subjects of mutual interest, and what scope we have for conjecture as to how their hidden souls leaped out to meet each other !* The freed imagination lingers over such a meeting

* "I have seen Emerson," writes George Eliot to a friend with all the jubilant recollection of a genuine red-letter day—"1 have seen Emerson— the first *man* I have ever seen."

for days and seasons. We live again, for ourselves, the hours they thus lived, or should have lived, during that interview ; we hear again the words they spoke, or should have spoken ; and these help to make for us a life, nay, a world, sacred and personal and secluded. And what if such interviews, of which we write, were not all our fond fancy would have them be ! *They are enough for us as we make them, and we are content.*

One other point, not wholly insignificant : to enjoy with anything like thoroughness the " Interviews " between the notable personages whose names will be found scattered along the following pages, our readers must bring with them something of the hero-worship felt by Thackeray when he said : " I should like to have been Shakespeare's shoe-black, just to have lived in his house, just to have worshipped him, to have run on his errands, and seen that sweet, serene face."* Surely such a love as this was, in itself, a liberal education.

It does not matter how much superior to the worshipper the hero may be: the man who worships cannot fail to feel himself, in a certain sense, of kin to the object of his adoration. The mere act of worship has in itself an uplifting and refining influence of no mean extent.† In this higher life we repeat, in however crooked a fashion, the lives of the great whose sayings and doings we ponder over. The glimpses left to us

* Thackeray also liked to find indications of this spirit of hero-worship in others. "One day he was walking along Wych Street, a kind of slum-thoroughfare leading to Drury Lane, when he passed a group of dirty little street-arabs. One little female tatterdemalion looked up at him as he passed, and then called out to her younger brother, 'Hi, Archie! d'you know who him is? He's Becky Sharp.'"

† We draw the line, however, at conduct similar to that of the Duchess of Marlborough, who, after Congreve's death, is said to have preserved his memory by inviting to her table, as a constant guest, an automaton model of him in ivory.

in the recordings of their friends are as so many gaps in the hedge through which we peer in upon the paths they trod.*   Through imaginative sympathy we become immediate participators in the dramas in which they acted.   Our interest in the matter is thus as highly strung and intense as that of any artist in his creations—as intense, for instance, as that once shown by Thackeray, the story of which will bear repetition as illustrative of our meaning.   It is related that one day while *The Newcomes* was in course of publication, Lowell, who was then in London, met Thackeray on the street.   " The novelist was serious in manner, and his looks and voice told

* " The authors truly remembered and loved are *men* in the best sense of the term ; the human, the individual, informs and stamps their books with an image or an effluence not born of will or mere ingenuity, but emanating from the soul ; and this is the quality that endears and perpetuates their fame."—*Tuckerman.*

of weariness and affliction. He saw the kindly inquiry in the poet's eyes, and said : ' Come into Evans's, and I'll tell you all about it. *I have killed the Colonel !'** So they walked in and took a table in a remote corner ; and then Thackeray, drawing the fresh manuscript from his breast-pocket,

---

* Walter Herries Pollock tells us an anecdote of Anthony Trollope which is curious and characteristic. " He was by no means," says Pollock, " given to talking of his own accord about his own works, past and present ; indeed, I do not remember to have ever heard him do so except on this occasion, when he was writing *The Last Chronicle of Barset*, and he took an opportunity of observing that there was an end of Mrs. Proudie. Being asked why, he replied that he had been writing in the —— Club, and that round the fireplace in the room there was gathered a group of young clergymen. They were talking about *The Last Chronicle*, and it was impossible for him to avoid hearing what they said. They spoke of the work in high praise, but they all agreed as to one point—that Mrs. Proudie was becoming an intolerable nuisance. ' What did you do ?' we asked. ' Well,' he replied, ' I hesitated a good deal what to do. But I finally made up my mind, and went up to them and explained that I couldn't help hearing what they were saying, and I added : "I'm very much obliged to you. I am Anthony Trollope, and I'll go home at once and kill Mrs. Proudie." ' And he did.

2

read through that exquisitely touching chapter which records the death of Colonel Newcome. When he came to the final *Adsum*, the tears which had been swelling his lids for some time trickled down his face, and the last word was almost an inarticulate sob."*

* In some recently-published reminiscences of Thackeray, Mr. C. P. Cranch relates his having met him in London in 1855. "At an adjournment after dinner to the ʻCider Cellarʼ—a very plainly-furnished but comfortable parlour on the first-floor—Thackeray said to the company : ʻ By the way, have you seen the last number of *The Newcomes ?*ʼ

"The company said they had not.

" ʻThen,ʼ said Thackeray, ʻ I should very much like to read you some of it. It is just out.ʼ We all, of course, says Mr. Cranch, expressed an eager pleasure in this opportunity of hearing him read anything from his own books. Whereupon he summoned a waiter, and said:

" ʻ Here, waiter—here's a shilling—I want you to go out and buy for me the last number of *The Newcomes.*ʼ

" It was soon brought ; and Thackeray began to read, and read for an hour, I should think, in his quiet, half-plaintive voice, some of the closing scenes in his novel. We were all deeply interested. I think the last page he read described the death-bed of Colonel Newcome. . . . I have recorded this meeting exactly as it occurred, as there has been another version published, not quite correct."

And yet another instance, perhaps not so well known, of this finer sympathy, this absolute surrender of self to what is unseen, but none the less thoroughly realized. " One day Mrs. Henry Siddons, a neighbour and intimate of Lord Jeffrey, who often entered his library unannounced, opened the door very gently to see if he were there, and saw enough at a glance to convince her that the visit was ill-timed. The hard critic of the *Edinburgh Review* was sitting in his chair with his head on the table in deep grief. As Mrs. Siddons was retiring, in the hope that her entrance had been unnoticed, Jeffrey raised his head and kindly beckoned her back. Perceiving that his cheek was flushed, and his eyes suffused with tears, she begged permission to withdraw. When he found that she was intending to leave him, he rose from

2—2

his chair, took her by both hands, and led her to a seat.

" ' Don't go, my dear friend; I shall be right again in another minute.'

" ' I had no idea you had had any bad news, or cause for grief, or I would not have come. Is anyone dead ?'

" ' Yes, indeed. I'm a great goose to have given way so, but I could not help it. You'll be sorry to hear that little Nelly—Boz's little Nelly— is dead.' "

Trifles like these often possess a distinct value of their own; and, after all, " it is only by the light of the tittle-tattle of tradition that we can stroll along Fleet Street with Dr. Johnson to the Mitre Tavern, or to the Kit-Cat to meet Burke, and Gibbon, and Goldsmith; spend half an hour with Cowper in his workshop ; or walk down the High

Street of Edinburgh with Professor Wilson to his class-room, 'with a book under his arm and a week's beard on his chin.'"

Surely the gist of the whole matter of which we write is admirably expressed in the words of Victor Cousin : "If beauty, absent and dreamed of, does not affect you as much as, and more than, present beauty, you may have a thousand other gifts—that of imagination has been refused you."

Landor once said that most things were real to him except realities: and this we can well understand from several incidents in his life—all notable interviews, by the way, and with literary men too. One such will suffice for the present. When troubles hung thickly around him on account of his foolish conduct in the matter of the Bath scandal ; when his personal property had been all sold and his real estate transferred to his eldest son, and he was being hurried off to the Continent by his friends, he " arrived suddenly at Mr. Forster's house, where Dickens and some others were at dinner. Dickens left the table to see him, expecting naturally to find him broken and cast down. But the old man's thoughts were far away ; he seemed as though no ugly or infuriating realities had any existence for him, and sat talking in his most genial vein, principally *about Latin Poetry*."*

" I would not blot him out, in his tender gallantry, as he sat upon his bed at Forster's that night," said one of his friends, " for a million wild mistakes at eighty-four years of age."

If there really is but a thin partition between great wit and madness, then is one to be often pardoned for an unjust estimate of a great man.

* Colvin's *Landor*.

Take, for instance, the first appearance of Jonathan Swift on the scene where afterwards he was to be the moving spirit. We are introduced to him at the famous coffee-house in Covent Garden kept by Button, and frequented by the gentlemen who were termed " the wits." These wits, one of them tells us, had for several successive days observed in the coffee-house a strange clergyman, who seemed utterly unacquainted with any of them, and whose custom it was to lay his hat down on a table, and " walk backward and forward at a good pace for half an hour, or an hour, without speaking to any mortal, or seeming in the least to attend to anything that was going forward there. He then used to take up his hat, pay his money at the bar, and walk away without opening his lips." The onlookers, as may be supposed, were greatly fluttered by the apparition; for, "having observed his singular behaviour for some time, they concluded him to be out of his senses, and the name that he went by among them was that of 'The Mad Parson.'" One evening, as Mr. Addison and the rest of the wits were observing this strange character, they saw him cast his eyes several times on "a gentleman in boots, who seemed to be just come out of the country;" and at last, "in a very abrupt manner, without any previous salute"—for Swift even then did not fashion himself to the formalities—"asked him if he remembered any good weather in the world." The gentleman in boots, after staring a little at the oddity of the question, answered that he "remembered a great deal." "That is more than I can say," rejoined the questioner. "I never remember any that was not too hot or too cold, too wet or too dry. But, however God Almighty contrives it, at the end of the year it is all very well."* The spectators of this scene, who had quitted their seats to get nearer the interlocutors, were, we are told, more than ever confirmed in their opinion of the strange parson's madness.

* *Literature and its Professors*, by Thomas Purnell.

II.

TOWARDS THE INFINITE.

" The ancient Aryans felt from the beginning, ay, it may be, more in the beginning than afterwards, the presence of a Beyond, of an Infinite, of a Divine, or whatever else we may call it now ; and they tried to grasp and comprehend it, as we all do, by giving to it name after name. . . . They forsook the bright Devas, not because they believed or desired less, but because they believed and desired more than the bright Devas. There was a new conception working in their mind ; and the cries of despair were but the harbingers of a new birth."—MAX MÜLLER : "On the Origin and Growth of Religion as illustrated by the Religions of India."

" Mystical, more than magical, is that Communing of Soul with Soul, both looking heavenward : here properly Soul first speaks with Soul."—CARLYLE : "Sartor Resartus."

THIS age of ours is certainly one of mental unrest. Everyone has views and aspirations of his own

on all subjects, from the earth-
worm to the over-soul. Doubt of
some kind or other generally runs
in harness with these views and
aspirations, or rather, usually pre-
cedes them. It is sometimes of
a low and frivolous character, pretentious and boasting, blowing a
trumpet to indicate its existence.
The doubter says to himself in
foolish pride : " The greatest men of
the age are unbelievers, and I will
be one, for I, too, am superior
to the common herd." Alas, poor
fool ! Why not drive a thoroughly
logical conclusion, and say : " The
greatest singers of the day, Tennyson, Browning, and two or three
others, fasten their boots with tagged
laces, and so do I ; therefore I, too,
am a great singer."

But to the man of tender, yet
strong, nature, whose desire to get
nearer his God is the hunger and

thirst of his life, and who, in his
struggle to that end, has to cast
aside some of the accumulated ideas
of centuries on minor points ; who,
whilst floundering in mental uncertainty, still keeps his heart pure and
turned to the white light of God's
presence in the soul ; who, whilst
surrounded by slighting looks and
pitying shoulder-shrugs, can sit tran-
quilly by his own hearthstone and
croon to himself such an intense
throb as Newman's " Lead, Kindly
Light "—to such an one God's smile
goes out, and the strong heart-grip of
the noblest men now living on this
dear earth of ours.

I wish to write no deification of
doubt : rather would I sing of the
quiet lanes where restful trust wan-
ders content—where heaven's sunshine falls through the green leaves
overhead, and the song of the soaring
lark is heard. But the manly utter-

ances of Max Müller, in his *Hibbert Lectures*, ring again and again in our ears, teaching us not only lessons of sympathy and brotherliness, but also of reliance on some of the ways of the soul. "Now I know perfectly well," he said in one of those notable discourses, delivered in the Chapter House of Westminster Abbey, "that what I have said just now will be misunderstood, will possibly be misinterpreted. I know I shall be accused of having defended and glorified atheism, and of having represented it as the last and highest point which man can reach in an evolution of religious thought. Let it be so! If there are but a few here present who understand what I mean by honest atheism, and who know how it differs from vulgar atheism—ay, from dishonest theism, I shall feel satisfied; for I know that to understand that distinction will often help us in the hour of our sorest need. It will teach us that, while the old leaves— the leaves of a bright and happy spring—are falling, and all seems wintry, frozen, and dead, within and around us there is, and there must be, a new spring in store for every warm and honest heart. It will teach us that honest doubt is the deepest spring of honest faith ; and that he only who has lost can find."

In this connection we cannot, of course, fail to remember the memorable occasion of Emerson's visit to Carlyle at Craigenputtock, when they went out together on the brown hills, and sat down and talked of the immortality of the soul. " I came," wrote Emerson some time afterwards, " from Glasgow to Dumfries, and being intent on delivering a letter which I had brought from Rome, inquired for Craigenputtock. It was a farm in Nithsdale, in the parish of Dunscore, sixteen miles distant. No public coach passed near it, so I took a private carriage from the inn. I found the house amid desolate heathery hills, where the lonely scholar nourished his mighty heart. Carlyle was a man from his youth, an author who did not need to hide from his readers, and as absolute a man of the world, unknown and exiled on that hill-farm, as if holding in his own terms what is best in London. He was tall and gaunt, with a cliff-like brow, self-possessed, and holding his extraordinary powers of conversation in easy command; clinging to his northern accent with evident relish; full of lively anecdote, and with a streaming humour which floated everything he looked upon. . . . Few were the objects, and lonely the man —'not a person to speak to within sixteen miles except the minister of

Dunscore '—so that books inevitably
made his topics. . . . We went out
to walk over the long hills, and
looked at Criffel, then without his
cap, and down into Wordsworth's
country. *There we sat down and
talked of the immortality of the soul.*"

This "talk" must be to us solely of
our own liking and formation, based
upon what we can glean of the views
of these two friends; for what else on
this point is given us by Emerson is
vague and suggestive only. " It was
not Carlyle's fault," he continues,
" that we talked on that topic, for
he had the natural disinclination of
every nimble spirit to bruise itself
against walls, and did not like to
place himself where no steps can be
taken. But he was honest and true,
and cognisant of the subtle links that
bind ages together, and saw how
every event affects all the future.
' Christ died on the tree : that built

Dunscore kirk yonder: that brought you and me together. Time has only a relative existence.'"

What a subject is thus opened up for speculation! I remember as a youth reading and re-reading the account of this meeting, and piecing together in my mind the lines which possibly might have been taken by the talkers. All the charm of that early endeavour "to force by conjecture a passage into other people's thoughts" recurs to me as I write the simple words which still have the old-time, mystical music about them : " *There we sat down and talked of the immortality of the soul.*"*

* Carlyle referred with enthusiasm to this meeting, and of their "quiet night of clear, fine talk." He spoke lovingly of the day " when that supernal vision, Waldo Emerson, dawned on him."

It is currently reported that Carlyle liked to remember that other evening, in London, on which Tennyson and he sat in solemn silence smoking for hours. "Man Alfred," said Carlyle, as he bade his visitor good-night, "we have ha'en a graund nicht ; come back again soon !"

3

Years afterwards, when Emerson again visited Carlyle, it is said that they sat by themselves a goodly portion of the evening, in the dark, talking only of God and immortality, as if anxious to discover whether their philosophy had thrown any clearer light on the all-absorbing topics discussed by them on the Scotch hills.*

At Kirkcaldy, long before this, Carlyle had made, or strengthened, an acquaintance with Edward Irving, like himself an Annandale man, like himself a student of divinity, and, once more, like himself, a teacher in a Kirkcaldy school. "By residents in Kirkcaldy," says Dix, "I

---

* "I must tell you a story Miss Bremer got from Emerson. Carlyle was very angry with him for not believing in a devil, and to convert him took him amongst all the horrors of London—the gin-shops, etc.—and finally to the House of Commons, plying him at every turn with the question, 'Do you believe in a devil noo?'"—*George Eliot to Sara Hennell*, 3rd Nov., 1851.

have heard the two described as often seen walking on the sea-beach in earnest conversation, and no doubt the doctrines of the Church, which both were preparing to enter, formed frequently a main portion of their talk, to which it would not be surprising if Carlyle contributed the sceptical, and Irving the believing, portion. It is curious that both these men should afterwards have made so very peculiar a figure in London, as stormy denouncers (each in his own fashion) of the established present, and prophets of a better future."*

* What Carlyle wrote as an epitaph on Irving came forth hot and earnest, and direct from his heart. " He referred to his short life (forty-two years only)—of his thorough truth, of his youth maturing in the Scotch solitudes—and, after abiding for a time in the cold northern city, of his being cast into this blazing Babylon, where he was at first smothered with caresses, and then denounced by the fickle, veering idolaters who crawled at his feet. Yet not a fact could be urged against him, except that his opinions differed from theirs. So they cast him down into the satanic pit, amongst

As I look out just now from my study window upon the stars, steel-blue above the downs, my thoughts are carried away to another meeting (or, rather, break-up of a meeting), at which Carlyle took his part. I know right well that these stories of the Chelsea Sage are common property with all readers ; but they suit my mood and purpose, and I use them accordingly, though not to fill the pages of this little volume with padding.*   Soon after the publica-

---

the refuse of their kind, and went on worshipping another image—some coarse Belial whom they had themselves manufactured, and transfigured into a god."

* There seems to me nothing in our literature more full of genuine human feeling, unparaded as it is, than the following, extracted from Carlyle's *Life of John Sterling. The man Carlyle, at his best, is in it.*   " But now," he says, " autumn approaching, Sterling had to quit clubs for matters of sadder consideration.   A new removal, what we call ' his third peregrinity,' had to be decided on ; and it was resolved that Rome should be the goal of it, the journey to be done in company with Calvert, whom, also, the Italian climate might be made to serve instead of Madeira.   One of the

tion of *Heroes and Hero-Worship*, Carlyle and Leigh Hunt were together at a small party, and a conversation was started between these two concerning the heroism of man. "Leigh Hunt had said something about the islands of the blest, or El Dorado, or the Millennium, and was flowing on his bright and hopeful

---

liveliest recollections I have, connected with the *Anonymous Club* [a little club, established by John Sterling, where monthly, over a frugal dinner, a small select company of persons, to whom it was pleasant to talk, used to meet, having Tennyson as one of the number, and James Spedding for secretary], is that of once escorting Sterling, after a certain meeting there, which I had seen only towards the end, and now remember nothing of, except that, on breaking up, he proved to be encumbered with a carpet-bag, and could not at once find a cab for Knightsbridge. Some little bantering hereupon, during the instants of embargo. But we carried his carpet-bag, slinging it on my stick, two or three of us alternately, through dusty vacant streets, under the gaslight and the stars, towards the surest cab-stand, still jesting, or pretending to jest, he and we, not in the mirthfulest manner, and had (I suppose) our own feelings about the poor pilgrim, who was to go on the morrow, and had hurried to meet us in this way, as the last thing before leaving England."

way, when Carlyle dropped some
heavy tree-trunk across Hunt's pleasant stream, and banked it up with
philosophical doubts and objections
at every interval of the speaker's
joyous progress.   But the unmiti-
gated Hunt never ceased his over-
flowing anticipations, nor the satur-
nine Carlyle his infinite demurs to
these finite flourishings.   The lis-
teners laughed and applauded by
turns, and had now fairly pitted
them against each other as the
philosopher of hopefulness and of
the unhopeful.   The contest continued with all that ready wit and
philosophy, that mixture of plea-
santry and profundity, that extensive knowledge of books and character, with their ready application in
argument or illustration, and that
perfect ease and good-nature which
distinguished both of these men.
The opponents were so well matched

that it was quite clear the contest would never come to an end. But the night was far advanced, and the party broke up. They all sallied forth, and, leaving the close room, the candles and the arguments behind them, suddenly found themselves in presence of a most brilliant star-lit night. They all looked up. 'Now,' thought Hunt, 'Carlyle's done for! He can have no answer to that!'

"'There!' shouted Hunt; 'look up there—look at that glorious harmony, that sings with infinite voices an eternal song of hope in the soul of man.'

"Carlyle looked up. They all remained silent to hear what he would say. They began to think he was silenced at last; he was a mortal man. But out of that silence came a few low-toned words, in a broad Scotch accent. And who on earth could have anticipated what the voice said ?

" ' Eh, it's a sad sight !'

" Hunt sat down on a stone step. They all laughed, then looked very thoughtful. Had the finite measured itself with infinity, instead of surrendering itself up to the influence ? Again they laughed, then bade each other good-night, and betook themselves homewards with slow and serious pace."*

How different to all this were the conversations on the same all-absorbing topics which took place between Baxter and Sir Matthew Hale, of

---

* Horne's *New Spirit of the Age.*
What a right lovable and kindly spirit had Leigh Hunt ! After a dinner at the house of Barry Cornwall, at which Kinglake and Hawthorne, amongst others, were present, when the gentlemen rose to join the ladies in the drawing-room, " the two dear old poets, Leigh Hunt and Barry Cornwall, mounted the stairs with their arms round each other in a very tender and loving way. Hawthorne often referred to this scene as one he would not have missed for a great deal."

which the former tells us : "The conference which I had frequently with him, mostly about the immortality of the soul and other philosophical and foundation points, was so edifying that his very questions and objections did help me to more light than other men's solutions."

Mr. F. W. H. Myers, in an extremely interesting article on George Eliot, tells of how he once walked with her at Cambridge, in the Fellows' garden of Trinity, on an evening of rainy May, when "she, stirred somewhat beyond her wont, and taking as her text the three words which have been used so often as the inspiring trumpet - calls of men — the words *God, Immortality, Duty* — pronounced with terrible earnestness how inconceivable was the *first*, how unbelievable the *second*, and yet how peremptory and absolute the *third*. Never, perhaps," he continues, "have sterner accents affirmed the sovereignty of impersonal and unrecompensing law. I listened, and night fell ; her grave, majestic countenance turned toward me like a sibyl's in the gloom ; it was as though she withdrew from my grasp one by one the two scrolls of promise, and left me the third scroll only, awful with inevitable fates. And when we stood at length and parted, amid that columnar circuit of the forest trees, beneath the last twilight of starless skies, I seemed to be gazing, like Titus at Jerusalem, on vacant seats and empty halls—on a sanctuary with no presence to hallow it, and heaven left lonely of a God."

To many noble-hearted men and women, even nowadays, nothing is left but their duty. Through some defect in their soul's sight they fail to see the ultimate of the busy speculation with which this nine-

teenth century is rife — nay, they
scarce see even its true tendency.
Its way is so devious; and the maze
through which it subtly glides is so
overgrown and difficult of penetra-
tion, that it is a matter of no wonder
that a shrewd conjecture is often
made to take the place of definite
knowledge. But work is definite
and always near at hand—something
upon which energy can be legiti-
mately expended, and from which
results can be calculated with pre-
cision. And the truth remains ever
fresh, that "to forget yourself in some
worthy purpose outside of yourself
is the secret of a rich and happy
life." Many a man, wrapped round
with the coils of black doubt, can,
equally with him who lives in the
sunshine of faith, set his seal to the
truth of what has been written of
the glory of true work earnestly per-
formed. I say *true work earnestly per-*

formed, having in my mind the saying of Emerson: "God will not have His work made manifest by cowards. A man is relieved and gay when he has put his heart into his work and done his best; but what he has said or done otherwise shall give him no peace. It is a deliverance which does not deliver. In the attempt his genius deserts him; no muse befriends; no invention, no hope."

I should like to have seen the grim visage of Carlyle, and the play upon the features of William Black the novelist, at that interview when the Chelsea Sage put the posing question to his younger brother of the pen who, by the way, has given us such charming stories: "But when are ye going to do some *wark?*"*

* Mr. Carlyle's severest critic, and a critic of his own school, was an old parish roadman at Ecclefechan.

"Been a long time in this neighbourhood?" once asked an American traveller on the outlook for a sight of the sage.

In these days of raving about genius and its prescriptive rights of vagabondage and irresponsibility, it is refreshing to read the definite statements made about work, even though the sentiment be common-place and has found a home in every

---

"Been here a' ma days, sir."

"Then you'll know the Carlyles?"

"Weel that ! A ken the whole o' thèm. There was, let me see," he said, leaning on his shovel and pondering, "there was Jock ; he was a kind o' throughither sort o' chap, a doctor, but no a bad fellow, Jock—he's deid, mon."

"And there was Thomas," said the inquirer eagerly.

"Oh, ay, of coorse, there's Tam—a useless, munestruck chap that writes in London. There's naething in Tam ; but, mon, there's Jamie, owre in the Newlands--there's a chap for ye ; he's the mon o' the family. Jamie tak's maire swine into Ecclefechan market than any ither farmer in the parish."

This is all very much like the story of the Scottish driver of pigs, who, hearing it declared that he was a greater man than the Duke of Wellington, scratched his thick head, and with a satisfied ex-pression said : "Aweel, Wellington was a great mon, and verra smart in his own way ; but I doot —I doot, if *he* could ha' driven seven hundred pigs frae Edinboro to Lonnon—and not lose one —as *I* ha' done."

teacher's exhortation. There is a genuine ring about such as the following: "Work every hour, paid or unpaid; see only that you work, and you cannot escape your reward. Whether your work be fine or coarse, planting corn or writing epics, so only it be honest work, done to your own approbation, it shall earn a reward to the senses as well as to the thought. No matter how often defeated, you are born to victory. The reward of a thing well done is to have done it."

III.

MUTUAL-ADMIRATION SOCIETIES.

" We had experience of a blissful state,
In which our powers of thought stood separate,
Each in its own high freedom held apart,
Yet both close folded in one loving heart ;
So that we seemed, without conceit, to be
Both one, and two, in our identity."
MILNES.

" Genius without sympathetic recognition is like
a kindled fire without flue or draught ; it smoulders
miserably away instead of leaping, sparkling, and
giving cheer."—BAYARD TAYLOR.

" Gaze thou in the face of thy brother, in those
eyes where plays the lambent fire of kindness . . .
feel how thy own so quiet soul is straightway in-
voluntarily kindled with the like, and ye blaze and
reverberate on each other, till it is all one limitless
confluent flame . . . and then say what miraculous
virtue goes out of man into man."—CARLYLE.

NOTHING tends more to lay a man's
soul bare than to have a sympathetic
listener or two. The world's cold

criticism is all forgotten in the presence of friendly hearts and answering eyes. These conditions are often found by the world's workers in select clubs,* where man meets man without formality or restraint of any kind; where he expects to find, and generally does find, in his brother something admirable and charming.† And "if they are men

---

* To attempt to exhaust the subject of clubs in a little book like the present would, it need hardly be said, prove something akin to gathering the hills together to stow in a barn. Volumes might be written in this direction, and yet much would be left unrecorded. To start even with the picture of an evening at the Globe with Kit Marlowe (alas, poor Kit!—"Christopher Marlowe, slain by a serving-man in a drunken brawl, aged twenty-nine") and Shakespeare, Cowley and Green, Ned Alleyn, George Peele, Nash, and the rest of the merry crew, all in a storm of inspiration and drink, would open up untold chapters in the literary history of England.

† And this, notwithstanding Charlotte Brontë's opinion on the matter. "All coteries," she says in one of her letters, "whether they be literary, scientific, political, or religious, must, it seems to me, have a tendency to change truth into affectation. When people belong to a clique, they must, I suppose, in some measure, write, talk, think, and live for that clique—a harassing and narrowing necessity."

with noble powers and qualities, let me tell you that, next to youthful love and family affections, there is no human sentiment better than that which unites the societies of mutual admiration. And what would literature or art be without such associations? Who can tell what we owe to the Mutual Admiration Society of which Shakespeare and Ben Jonson, and Beaumont and Fletcher were members? Or to that of which Addison and Steele formed the centre, and which gave us the *Spectator?* Or to that where Johnson and Goldsmith, and Burke and Reynolds, and Beauclerk and Boswell, most admiring among all admirers, met together?*

* "Who has not heard of the famous lobster suppers of Pope, and the witty re-unions at Tom's Coffee House, where ruffled and rapiered gallants met to discuss liquor and literature, chat and claret? or, who has not longed to make one of such a party as that described, or rather referred to, by the sprightly Lady Mary Wortley Montague, who, with chosen associates,

"'When the cares of the day are all pass'd
   Sit down with champagne and a chicken at last;'

4

Was there any great harm in the
fact that the Irvings and Pauld-

and to what was far better,—'the feast of reason
and the flow of soul.' These 'long-ago' affairs
have had their Boswells to chronicle them ; and
so graphic are some of the reports of these
symposia, that we seem, whilst perusing them, to
' live over each scene.' In imagination we jostle
against flower-brocaded coats and embroidered
vests ; our modern legs get entangled in the
voluminous folds of the ample fardingales and
hoops, and high heels startle us with their grotesque
proportions.

"The times have changed ; the days of the
blue-stocking clique are remembered as among the
things that were. Hannah More, Mrs. Delaney,
Mrs. Thrale, Mrs. Piozzi, and Madame D'Arblay
no longer sit sipping their souchong, and listening
to the oracular and ponderous sentences of Doctor
Johnson, or indulging in sprightly sentimentalisms,
or flippant nothings. Will's coffee-house is no
longer open to the Steeles, the Addisons, and the rest
of the town wits. Tom's exists, but is a lawyer's
dining-house. Ranelagh, with its variegated
leafy arcades, and brilliantly-lighted bowers, is no
more ; and all who gossiped so delightfully, or
talked so learnedly, a few years ago, have passed
away, leaving legacies of wit, wisdom and folly to
their descendants, who, in the cockney haunts of
Rosherville and Cremorne, make up for the almost
forsaken glories of Vauxhall—that latest remnant
of old-fashioned gaiety.

"The times have greatly changed. Club-houses
have knocked the old coffee-houses into nothing-
ness ; and literary coteries are broken up—*such*
literary coteries, we mean, as the days to which
reference has been made could boast of."—DIX's
Lions Living and Dead.

ing wrote in company? or any un-
pardonable cabal in the literary
union of Verplanck and Bryant and
Sands, and as many more as they
chose to associate with them?

" The poor creature does not
know what he is talking about when
he abuses this noblest of institutions.
Let him inspect its mysteries through
the knot-hole he has secured, but
not use that orifice as a medium for
his popgun. Such a society is the
crown of a literary metropolis; if a
town has not material for it, and
spirit and good feeling enough to
organize it, it is a mere caravansary,
fit for a man of genius to lodge in,
but not to live in. Foolish people
hate and dread and envy such an
association of men of varied powers
and influence, because it is lofty,
serene, impregnable, and, by the
necessity of the case, exclusive.
Wise ones are prouder of the title

4—2

M.S.M.A., than of all their other honours put together."*

And no small portion of the record of what is best in literature is also a history of cliques, in which the workers helped each other by mutual criticism as well as by mutual admiration. In the very nature of events, one strong or beautiful soul must needs, by virtue of its magnetism, draw to itself others of similar character.

What notable gatherings and conferences it is possible to construct imaginatively when we have as a basis for our operations the names of the contributors to the first number of the *Edinburgh Review*, together with some odd particulars, now tolerably well known, of how the famous quarterly was started and pushed out on its early way among men ! And what a chant of

---

* Oliver Wendell Holmes.—*The Autocrat of the Breakfast Table.*

the wealth of intellect these names
sing for themselves ! Here they are :
Francis (afterwards Lord) Jeffrey ;
Henry Brougham, subsequently Lord
Brougham ; Alexander Hamilton,
sometime Professor of Sanscrit in
the East India College at Haileybury;
Francis Horner, known to the reading public through his memoirs
edited by his brother ; Sydney Smith,
" the witty parson," with his untied
tongue ; John Macfarlan, the serious,
studious, and retired lover of German
and metaphysics; Dr. John Thomson,
who occupied some years afterwards
the chair of pathology in the College
of Edinburgh ; Dr. Thomas Brown ;
and John Murray, afterwards Lord
Murray, a judge.

Of these in 1802 (the date of the
publication of the first number of
the *Edinburgh*), Smith was thirty-
one years of age ; Jeffrey, thirty ;

Brown, twenty-four; Horner, twenty-four; and Brougham, twenty-three.

These are the men with whom we live again the life they spent during the few months surrounding the issue of the first number of their *Review*, concerning which it has been said: "The effect was electrical. . . . It is impossible for those who did not live at the time, and in the heart of the scene, to feel, or almost to understand, the impression made by the new luminary, or the anxieties with which its motions were observed. It was an entire and instant change of everything that the public had been accustomed to in that sort of composition. The old periodical opiates were extinguished at once."

Willis once said, in the course of conversation with G. W. Curtis, that people always read with avidity two things—stories of themselves and of other people. The story of the

inception and early existence of the
Edinburgh Review, however often repeated, is certainly one to be read
with interest by all students of
literary history. The plain facts are
to be stated in few words. One
stormy night in March, 1802, a group
of friends met together in Jeffrey's
study (a room on the third story of a
house in Buccleuch Place, Edinburgh,
and called by courtesy his "study,"
the furnishing of which had been
completed at a cost of £7 18s.) to
consider their positions in life and
the means of bettering them. What
a goodly company gathered there
around their host! and what a storm
of laughter must have drowned the
storm without as one suggestion
after another fell from the lips of
Jeffrey, or Brougham, or Sydney
Smith, or Horner with the ten com-
mandments, as Smith used to say,
all written in the lines of his face

as legibly as they were on the tables of stone! Smith's story is (and it has been told also by Jeffrey and Brougham): " I proposed that we should set up a Review, and this was acceded to with acclamation. I was appointed editor, and remained long enough in Edinburgh to edit the first number of the *Edinburgh Review.*" The question arose as to a motto for the new publication. Smith suggested (and what else could be expected from such a man ?) that they should take " *Tenui Musam meditamur avenâ* " (" We cultivate literature on a little oatmeal "), but this was immediately ruled out of court, and for one of the best possible reasons; it was by far too near the truth to be blazed abroad from the house-tops. There was a copy of Publius Syrus lying on the table, and Horner, taking it up and turning over the leaves, accidentally

hit on the words which still occupy
their position on the old buff and
blue : " *Judex damnatur cum nocens
absolvitur !*" Subsequently Constable
was chosen as publisher, and the
papers in the first three numbers
were supplied him without remuneration. But the projectors of the *Review* knew right well the man with
whom they had to deal. Lord
Cockburn's estimate of him, in his
Memorials of his Time, is certainly a
pleasant picture. "Constable," he
writes, " had hardly set up for himself when he reached the summit of
his business. He rushed out and
took possession of the open field, as
if he had been aware from the first of
the existence of the latent spirits
which a skilful conjuror might call
from the depths of the population to
the service of literature. Abandoning
the old timid and grudging system,
he stood out as the general patron

and payer of all promising publications, and confounded, not merely his rivals in trade, but his very authors, by his unheard-of prices. Ten, even twenty, guineas a sheet for a review, £2,000 or £3,000 for a single poem, and £1,000 each for two philosophical dissertations,* drew authors from dens where they would otherwise have starved, and made Edinburgh a literary mart, famous with strangers and the pride of its own citizens."

Another picture, however, presents itself as companion to the meeting in Jeffrey's study, when the idea of such a publication was started. It is that of the writers skulking round back lanes to throw possible watchers off the scent before slipping quietly into "the dingy room off Wilkinson's printing-office, in Craig's Close,"

* By Stewart and Playfair—prefixed to a supplement of the *Encyclopædia Britannica.*

where they read over the proofs of their own articles, and sat in judgment on the few manuscripts offered by strangers. Sydney Smith gives us a peep at one of these meetings, where he and Brougham sat together over a glass of whisky to take the conceit out of some sapient author. " Once I remember," he says, " how we got hold of a little vegetarian, who had put out a silly little book ; and how Brougham and I sat one night over our review of that book, looking whether there was a chink or crevice through which we could filter one more drop of verjuice." Such a confession is really magnificent in its artlessness.

Although many incidents are on record having to do, in some measure, with the *Review* and its writers, much remains unwritten. But over what we actually have, as reliable information, our imagination broods, creating for us interviews and conversations which ought to have taken place, thus enabling us, each for himself, to grasp the romance which surrounds such an epoch in English literature.

Then there was that notable group which at one time gathered at the English lakes, and of which Wordsworth was the centre. " Here that strange being, Thomas de Quincey, came and lived, purposely to be near the poet. Coleridge* was always at call ; and loving and gentle Charles Lamb came at times, sadly missing the town, and almost afraid of the mountains. Here Dr. Arnold, of

* Landor was displeased with Coleridge altogether when he met him in London in 1832, although the philosopher donned a new suit of clothes for the occasion, and made many pretty speeches to his visitor. Landor's dislike was based upon two especial points : Coleridge would talk about no one and nothing but himself, and he would not pay the slightest attention to Landor's enthusiastic mention of Southey.

Rugby, came often from Fox How, his own house in the neighbourhood; hither Harriet Martineau walked over from Ambleside, with some new theory of the universe to expound ; and here poor Hartley Coleridge passed the happiest hours of his unfortunate life." And not far distant lived Southey in his magnificent library looking out on the everlasting hills.*

But we must by no means forget John Wilson, genial " Christopher North," certainly one of the most remarkable of the Lakists—" student, Bohemian, bookworm, sportsman, professor; the kindliest, merriest, and most entertaining of companions;" author of the *Noctes Ambrosianæ*.

---

* It was into this room that Southey one day enticed Shelley under the delusion that he had a treat for him ; and after locking the door dosed him with his verses until the would-be listener fell asleep under the table. He assured Shelley that his *Madoc* was equal to the *Odyssey*.

"In these same *Noctes* we have descriptions of some of those nights when, as Carlyle would have said, 'there was much good talk.' And Wilson was mainly the talker. The chief characteristics of his discourse were prodigality of humour and infinite variety. His imagination, too, ran riot, and his wit sparkled ever and anon with a radiance all its own.

"His memory was prodigious, and in his conversation he taxed it for anecdotes and illustrations drawn from the four quarters of the globe, and from the most remote and unusual stores of literary hoarding. His mind was many-sided as well as keen, and he kept all his faculties in full play, not excepting his sympathies, which were as broad as the world of men.

"Can we wonder that those who crowded the table where he sat lingered on till the daylight drove them from the board? or that no man who had had him for a boon companion could ever be satisfied with another? Can we wonder that the students who crowded his lecture-room after he became a professor thought every other lecturer common-place and dull? Not that he gave them more information than others —perhaps he did not give them as much; but he excited and inspired them. He quickened their minds, and wakened their dormant faculties. Some of the white-heat of his own enthusiasm he communicated to their colder natures, and they enjoyed the unusual warmth."*

* It was this power of inspiring and quickening that was so noticeable in Emerson's public utterances. James Russell Lowell says : " Emerson awakened us, saved us from the body of this death. It is the sound of the trumpet that the young soul longs for, careless what breath may fill it. Sidney heard it in the ballad of *Chevy Chase*, and we in Emerson. Nor did it blow retreat, but called to us with assurance of victory. Did they say he was disconnected? So were the stars, that seemed larger to our eyes, still keen with that ex-

"Wilson and De Quincey had been at Oxford together without acquaintance at the time. Wilson left college and settled at Elleray, by Lake Windermere, happy in a vigorous health and a fortune of thirty thousand pounds ; but happier some years later in the loss of the fortune; for it was that loss which brought his

---

citement, as we walked homeward with prouder stride over the creaking snow. And were *they* not knit together by a higher logic than our mere senses could master ? Were we enthusiasts ? I hope and believe we were, and am thankful to the man who made us worth something for once in our lives. If asked what was left ? what we carried home ? we should not have been careful for an answer. It would have been enough if we had said that something beautiful had passed that way. Or we might have asked in return what one brought away from a symphony of Beethoven ? Enough that he had set that ferment of wholesome discontent at work in us. There is one, at least, of those old hearers—so many of whom are now in the fruition of that intellectual beauty of which Emerson gave them both the desire and the foretaste—who will always love to repeat :

"' *Che in la mente m' è fitta, ed or m' accuora*
La cara e buona immagine paterna
Di voi, quando nel mondo ad ora ad ora
M'insegnavaste come l' uom s'eterna.' "

energies into full play. From 1809
Wilson, the tall, vigorous athlete,
with health in every movement of
his body and his mind, a man who
could jump twelve yards in three
jumps with a heavy stone in each
hand, became companion in rambles
with De Quincey, who was of under
height and slender of frame, with a
mind morbidly sensitive, not made
the healthier by use of opium.
The friendship between Thomas de
Quincey and John Wilson was life-
long. Each loved the poets, each
had his own touch of the sacred fire,
and the likeness in essentials was
accompanied with the complete un-
likeness in accidents of character that
fills one friend's life with ever-fresh
matter of study and enjoyment for
the other, and so doubles the experience of each."*

In the winter of 1814-15 De

* Henry Morley.

5

Quincey was with his friend Wilson in Edinburgh, where his silver stream of talk charmed all who heard it. "His voice," said one who met him then, "was extraordinary; it came as if from dreamland; but it was the most musical and impressive of voices. Seeing he was always good-natured and social, he could take part in any sort of tattle; but his musical cadences were not in keeping with such work, and in a few minutes (not without some strictly logical sequence) he could escape at will from beeves to butterflies, and thence to the soul's immortality, to Plato and Kant and Schelling and Fichte ; would recount profound mysteries from his own experiences —visions that had come over him in his loneliest walks among the mountains. And whatever the subject might be, every one of his sentences was woven into the most logical texture, and uttered in a tone of sustained melody."

In his *Personal Recollections of Thomas de Quincey*, John Ritchie Findlay refers in an interesting manner to a certain particular, in which the subject of his little volume undeniably resembled Coleridge. "He (De Quincey) had dined with me," writes Mr. Findlay, "at George Square; he preferred an early hour, and our small party had sat down to dinner at five or six o'clock. The two or three guests, all equally fascinated and delighted with his talk— only my uncle (Mr. John Ritchie, proprietor of the *Scotsman*; Mr. Russel being its editor), Russel and Burton probably—had left us one by one; my uncle for the country, where he was staying, I inhabiting alone his house in town; Burton unceremoniously enough when he thought fit to go; and at last Russel, about

eleven o'clock, he having his work at
the *Scotsman* office for next morning's
paper, as I had also. After fully an
hour more had slipped away, I was
obliged to tell De Quincey that I
too must go. Then came elegant
apologies, undoubtedly sincere, and
we left together, my desire being to
see him safe home to his lodgings in
Lothian Street. No ; he would ac-
company me through the silent midnight streets that fine summer evening. So we walked backwards and
forwards for probably another hour
between the High Street (where the
office of the *Scotsman* then was) and
Lothian Street, till at last the inevitable ' good-night ' was spoken. I got
to my post to find my work for the
night all but finished by Mr. Russel,
who immensely enjoyed the ' fix ' in
which he had left me, and was much
surprised at my having, by any device
or exercise of moral courage, got out

of it. As De Quincey said of Coleridge, that the first difficulty was to
get him to begin to talk, and the
second to get him to stop, so of De
Quincey, the first difficulty was to
induce him to visit you, and the
second to reconcile him to leaving."
Here to the region of the lake-poets
came the young Emerson, on his first
visit to England. " On the 28th
August, 1833," he says, " I went to
Rydal Mount to pay my respects to
Mr. Wordsworth.* His daughters

* When Wordsworth first went to reside in the
district, it was a matter of necessity with him that
the rule of his household should be " plain living
and high thinking." What friends came to see
him were always welcome to the bread and cheese
of his table ; if they needed more or better—well,
there was the village inn not far distant. Even
when his finances improved, the honest plainness
of his mode of living was apparent to all. We
are indebted to a communication by Mr. Jonathan
Bouchier to *Notes and Queries* for the following
story, which, in addition to being extremely
amusing in itself, illustrates the point to which we
have just referred :

"When Scott was staying with his friend and
brother-poet Wordsworth, the frugal fare—at least
in the article of liquor—at the bard of Rydal's

called in their father, a plain, elderly, white-haired man, not prepossessing, and disfigured by green goggles. He sat down, and talked with great simplicity. . . . I inquired if he had read Carlyle's critical articles and translations. He said he thought him sometimes insane. He proceeded to abuse Goethe's *Wilhelm Meister* heartily. He had never gone farther than the first part; so disgusted was he that he threw the book across the room. I deprecated his wrath, and said what I could for the better parts of the book, and he courteously promised

table did not quite suit Scott's less simple palate. He used, accordingly, to pay a visit to a neighbouring ' public,' and have a quiet glass, ' unbeknown,' as Mrs. Gamp would say, to Wordsworth. One day the two poets were walking out together, and they happened to pass the house, when the landlady was standing at the door. Directly she caught sight of Scott she exclaimed, to his horror, ' Weel, Mr. Scott, have ye come for your morning dram ?' thereby letting the cat out of the bag, and covering Scott with confusion."

to look at it again. Carlyle, he said, wrote most obscurely. He was clever and deep, but he defied the sympathies of everybody. Even Mr. Coleridge wrote more clearly, though he had always wished Coleridge would write more to be understood. He led me out into his garden, and showed me the gravel walk in which thousands of his lines were composed. His eyes are very much inflamed. This is no loss except for reading, because he never writes prose, and of poetry he carries even hundreds of lines in his head before writing them. He had just returned from a visit to Staffa, and within three days he had made three sonnets on Fingal's Cave, and was composing a fourth when he was called in to see me. He said: 'If you are interested in my verses, perhaps you will like to hear these lines.' I gladly assented, and he recollected himself for a few moments, and then stood forth and repeated one after the other the three entire sonnets with great animation. I fancied the second and third more beautiful than his poems are wont to be. The third is addressed to the flowers, which, he said, especially the ox-eye daisy, are very abundant on the top of the rock; the second alludes to the name of the cave, which is 'Cave of Music;' the first to the circumstance of its being visited by the promiscuous company of the steam-boat.

" This recitation was so unlooked for and surprising — he, the old Wordsworth, standing apart, and reciting to me in a garden-walk, like a school-boy declaiming—that I at first was near to laugh ; but recollecting myself that I had come thus far to see a poet, and he was chanting poems to me, I saw that he was right and I was wrong, and gladly gave myself up to hear. I told him how much the few printed extracts had quickened the desire to possess his unpublished poems. He replied he never was in haste to publish, partly because he corrected a good deal, and every alteration is ungraciously received after printing; but what he had written would be printed whether he lived or died. I said *Tintern Abbey* appeared to be the favourite poem with the public, but more contemplative readers preferred the first books of the *Excursion* and the *Sonnets.* He said, ' Yes, they are better.' He preferred such of his poems as touched the affections to any others; for whatever is didactic—what theories of society, and so on — might perish quickly, but whatever combined a truth with an affection was κτημα ες αει—good to-day and good for ever. He cited the sonnet, *On the feelings of a high-minded Spaniard*, which he preferred to any other (I so understood him), and the *Two Voices;* and quoted, with evident pleasure, the verses addressed *To the Skylark*."

It is remarkable in how many recorded interviews with the Rydal bard we find mention of his starting off with the recitation of his own verses; and it is curious to observe how differently the fact impresses his various hearers—some receiving the utterance reverently, others, and these mostly brother poets, turning restive under it as an infliction.

However one may admire Wordsworth, his egotism occasionally rubs up very roughly against our sensibilities. He told Lamb one day in the course of conversation that he considered Shakespeare greatly overrated.

" There is," said he, " an immen-

sity of trick in all Shakespeare wrote,
and people are taken by it. Now, if
I had a mind I could write exactly
like Shakespeare."

" Yes," stuttered Lamb in reply,
" it is only the mind that is wanting."

He once asked Mrs. Alaric Watts
what she thought the finest elegiac
composition in the English language,
and when she timidly suggested
Lycidas, he replied :

" You are not far wrong. It may,
I think, be affirmed that Milton's
Lycidas and my *Laodamia* are twin
immortals."

How very different was Lamb's
expressed estimate of himself! Calling on Wordsworth one day he
said :

" Mr. Wordsworth, allow me to
introduce to you my only admirer."

It was also a great pity that
Wordsworth was so very full of

"shop" on all occasions. If he had
been a little more niggardly in pour-
ing out his productions before his
visitors, it would have been better
for his reputation. "Enough is as
good as a feast." Dumas knew the
happy mean, and although such a
charming story-teller saw when to
draw the rein. One evening at a
party his hostess so wearied him with
requests to exhibit his powers in this
direction that at last, unable to en-
dure it longer, he quietly said:

"Everyone to his trade, madam.
The gentleman who entered your
drawing-room just before me is a
distinguished artillery officer. Let
him bring a cannon here and fire
it, then I will tell one of my little
stories."

I wonder what Byron really did
think of Coleridge when, on the very
first occasion of their meeting, he
treated the noble bard to one of his

interminable monologues wherein he ascended into the seventh heaven upon the wings of theology and metaphysics ! *

During his visit to England, Emerson called on Coleridge at Highgate, and they touched on theological amongst other subjects. I have no doubt his experience during the interview was very similar to Lamb's. One day Coleridge was regretting that Lamb had never heard him preach, whereupon Lamb retorted by saying that he had never heard him do anything else.

To Hazlitt, however, Coleridge's words were a revelation. In his essay on *My first Acquaintance with Poets*, speaking of his early meeting with Coleridge, he says :

* When Leigh Hunt, who was rather disgusted with Coleridge for his conduct on this occasion, related the story to Lamb, Lamb excused his friend by saying : "Oh, it was only his fun : there's an immense deal of quiet humour about Coleridge !"

" As we passed along between Wem and Shrewsbury . . . a sound was in my ears as of a siren's song; I was stunned, startled with it as from deep sleep, but I had no notion that I should ever be able to express my admiration to others in motley imagery or quaint allusion till the light of his genius shone into my soul like the sun's ray glittering in the puddles of the road. I was at that time dumb, inarticulate, help-less, like a worm by the wayside, crushed, bleeding, lifeless; but now, bursting the deadly bands that bound them,

" ' With Styx nine times round them,'

my ideas float on winged words, and as they expand their plumes, catch the golden light of other years. My soul has indeed remained in its original bondage, dark, obscure, with longings infinite and unsatisfied; my heart, shut up in the prison-house of this rude clay, has never found, nor will it ever find, a heart to speak to ;* but that my understanding also · did not remain dumb and brutish, or at length found a language to express itself, I owe to Coleridge.

" It was in January of 1798 that I rose one morning before daylight to walk ten miles in the mud to hear this celebrated person preach. Never,

---

* A rather comical commentary on these ex-pressions is afforded by Hazlitt's conduct, later in life, in the matter of the heroine of the *Liber Amoris* (Sarah Walker, the daughter of a lodging-house keeper), for whom he conceived an extra-vagant and altogether unreasonable passion which completely subdued his intellect. " He was, for a time," says Barry Cornwall, "unable to think or talk of anything else. He abandoned criticism and books as idle matters ; and fatigued every person whom he met by expressions of his love, of her deceit, and of his own vehement disap-pointment. This was when he lived in Southamp-ton Buildings, Holborn. Upon one occasion I know that he told the story of his attachment to five different persons in the same day, and at each time entered into minute details. 'I am a cursed fool,' said he to me. 'I saw J—— going into Will's Coffee-house yesterday morning ; he spoke to me. I followed him into the house ; and whilst he lunched, I told him the whole story.

the longest day I have to live, shall I
have such another walk as this cold,
raw, comfortless one in the winter.
. . . When I got there, the organ
was playing the 100th Psalm, and
when it was done, Mr. Coleridge rose
and gave out his text, 'And He went
up into the mountain to pray, HIM-
SELF, ALONE.' . . . . And for myself,
I could not have been more delighted
if I had heard the music of the
spheres. Poetry and philosophy

Then,' (said he) 'I wandered into Regent's
Park, where I met one of M——'s sons. I walked
with him some time, and on his using some civil
expression, by God! sir, I told him the whole
story.' [Here he mentioned another instance,
which I forget.] 'Well, sir' (he went on), 'I
then went and called on Haydon ; but he was
out. There was only his man, Salmon, there ;
but, by God! I could not help myself. It all
came out—the whole cursed story! Afterwards
I went to look at some lodgings at Pimlico. The
landlady at one place, after some explanations as
to rent, etc., said to me very kindly, " I am afraid
you are not well, sir ?" " No, ma'am," said I,
" I am not well ;" and on inquiring further, the
devil take me if I did not let out the whole story,
from beginning to end !'"

had met together. Truth and
genius had embraced under the
eye and with the sanction of religion. This was even beyond my
hopes. I returned home well satisfied. The sun that was still labouring pale and wan through the sky,
obscured by thick mists, seemed an
emblem of the *good cause;* and the
cold dank drops of dew, that hung
half melted on the beard of the
thistle, had something genial and
refreshing in them; for there was
a spirit of hope and youth in all
nature, that turned everything into
good. The face of nature had not
then the brand of Jus Divinum
on it :

"'Like to that sanguine flower inscribed with woe.'

" On the Tuesday following, the
half-inspired speaker came. I was
called down into the room where
he was, and went — half hoping,

6

half afraid. He received me very graciously, and I listened for a long time without uttering a word. I did not suffer in his opinion by my silence. 'For those two hours,' he afterwards was pleased to say, 'he was conversing with William Hazlitt's forehead.' "*

Then there was that notable group which once gathered around the *Atlantic Monthly !* Longfellow† and

---

* Madame de Staël, when once asked for her estimate of Coleridge, said: "He is great in monologue, but he has no idea of dialogue."

† On the publication of Longfellow's *Hiawatha,* the Boston *Daily Traveller* issued an adverse criticism of it, in which appeared the following: "His poem does not awaken one sympathetic throb; it does not teach a single truth; and rendered into prose, *Hiawatha* would be a mass of the most childish nonsense that ever dropped from human pen. In verse it contains nothing so precious as the golden time which would be lost in the reading of it."

Hereupon Messrs. Ticknor and Fields (Longfellow's publishers) wrote to the *Traveller,* withdrawing their advertisements, and asking to have the paper stopped; which had for a response the publication, in its completeness, of the missive, together with a sweet little commentary directly

Emerson; Whittier and Whipple; Holmes and Lowell, and Agassiz— "all the *beaux esprits* of the *Atlantic Monthly*, in a word; with an appropriate Corypheus in the person of Mr. James T. Fields, himself a ripe scholar, a poet of no mean order, and a 'funny fellow' to boot; for

---

charging the publishers with endeavouring to use all sorts of undue influence, etc.

"This," says F. H. Underwood, in his *Biographical Sketch of Longfellow*, "created no small stir; and as the poem at the same time was attacked on other grounds, the newspapers, from the Atlantic to the Mississippi, were soon engaged in a general controversy. Through all this storm Longfellow remained calm, paying no attention to assailants or defenders. It is said that Fields one day hurried off to Cambridge in a state of great excitement, that morning's mail having brought an unusually large batch of attacks and parodies, some of the charges being, he considered, of a seriously damaging character. 'My dear Mr. Longfellow,' he exclaimed, bursting into the poet's study, 'these atrocious libels must be stopped.' Longfellow glanced over the papers without comment. Handing them back, he quietly asked, 'By the way, Fields, how is *Hiawatha* selling?' 'Wonderfully!' replied the excited publisher; 'none of your books has ever had such a sale.' 'Then,' said the poet calmly, '*I think we had better let these people go on advertising it.*'"

6—2

he possessed a rich collection of New England witticisms and Yankee drolleries."* "Lowell and Holmes were the wits *par excellence,* though Judge Hoar did not fall far behind. Emerson sat always with a seraphic smile upon his face, and Longfellow thoroughly enjoyed every good sally, though not adding to the mirth-making himself."†

"Emerson was a member of the Saturday Club from the first—in reality before it existed as an empirical fact, and when it was only a platonic idea. The Club seems to have shaped itself around him as a nucleus of crystallization, two or three friends of his having first formed the habit of meeting him at dinner at 'Parker's,' the 'Will's Coffee-house' of Boston. This little group gathered others to itself and grew into a club, as Rome grew

* G. A. Sala. † H. T. Griswold.

into a city, almost without knowing
how. During its first decade the
Saturday Club brought together, as
members or as visitors, many distinguished persons. At one end of the
table sat Longfellow, florid, quiet,
benignant, soft-voiced—a most agreeable rather than a brilliant talker,
but a man upon whom it was always
pleasant to look—whose silence was
better than many another man's conversation. At the other end of the
table sat Agassiz, robust, sanguine,
animated, full of talk, boy-like in his
laughter. The stranger who should
have asked who were the men ranged
along the sides of the table would
have heard in answer the names of
Hawthorne,* Motley, Dana, Lowell,

---

* " It was only in the company of intimate personal friends, from whom all restraint was removed,
that Hawthorne ever indulged in his natural buoy-
ancy of spirits. Among them he occasionally
condescended to uproarious fun. But he was like
Dr. Johnson, who, when indulging in a scene of
wild hilarity, suddenly exclaimed to his friends,

Whipple ; Peirce, the distinguished mathematician; Judge Hoar, eminent at the Bar and in the Cabinet; Dwight, the leading musical critic of Boston for a whole generation ; Sumner, the academic champion of freedom ; Andrew, 'the great War Governor' of Massachusetts ; Dr. Howe, the philanthropist ; William Hunt, the painter, with others not unworthy of such company. And with these, generally near the Longfellow end of the table, sat Emerson, talking in low tones and carefully measured utterances to his neighbour, or listen- ing, and recording any stray word worth remembering on his mental phonograph. Emerson was a very regular attendant at the meeting of the Saturday Club, and continued to

---

as Beau Brummel approached, 'Let us be grave ; here comes a fool !' If there was the slightest suspicion of the presence of a fool in the company, Hawthorne always wore his armour."

dine at its table until within a year or two of his death."

This is Oliver Wendell Holmes' account, which he concludes by saying: "Unfortunately the Club had no Boswell, and its golden hours passed unrecorded."* And so we are driven back upon our old habit of availing ourselves of (to use the *Autocrat's* own words) "that blessed clairvoyance which sees into things without opening them—that glorious license, which, having shut the door and driven the reporter from its keyhole, calls upon Truth, majestic

---

* Once the Club dinner was given at Porter's hotel, "about a mile due north of the college in Cambridge;" and it was on this occasion that Longfellow, having just read Holmes' *new truth* that authors were like cats, sure to purr when stroked the right way of the fur, replied to some particular attention on the part of the *Autocrat* by saying, with a merry twinkle in his eyes, " I purr, I purr !" And then when the company broke up, and went out into the darkness, they found that during the evening a foot or more of snow had fallen ; so with arms linked, and the younger members singing Dr. Palmer's chorus *Puttyrum*, they tramped back to Cambridge.

virgin! to get off from her pedestal and drop her academic poses, and take a festive garland, and the vacant place on the *medius lectus* — that carnival-shower of questions and replies and comments, large axioms bowled over the mahogany like bomb-shells from professional mortars, and explosive wit dropping its trains of many-coloured fire, and the mischief rain of *bon-bons* pelting everybody that shows himself."

But when a man undertakes to paint his friends' portraits, he, too, must be content to sit for his own; so the Holmes omitted by Holmes is thus drawn by Dr. Appleton, who met him at the same brilliant gathering: " Dr. Holmes was highly talkative and agreeable; he converses very much like the *Autocrat of the Breakfast Table* — wittily, and in a literary way, but perhaps with too great an infusion of physiological and medical metaphor. He is a little deaf, and has a mouth like the beak of a bird; indeed, he is, with his small body and quick movements, very like a bird in his general aspect."

Occasionally, especially when in the presence of brilliant talkers and around the festive board, one is apt to over-shoot the mark, and to utter things which are afterwards severely reckoned up as " better unsaid." Mark Twain seems to have made a mistake of this kind at the banquet given to the contributors to the *Atlantic Monthly*, in celebration of Whittier's seventieth birthday. The irrepressible author of *The Jumping Frog*, was introduced by W. D. Howells as one " who has, perhaps, done more kindness to our race, lifted from it more crushing care, rescued it from more gloom, and banished from it more wretchedness,

than all the professional philan-
thropists that have lived; a humourist
who never makes you blush to have
enjoyed his joke; whose generous
wit has no bad meaning in it; whose
fun is never at the cost of anything
honestly high or good, but comes from
the soundest of hearts and the clearest
of heads."

Imagine the astonishment of the
refined and cultivated assembly when,
immediately following this, Mark
Twain arose, and, as C. M. Barrows*
relates, gave an account of the
unseemly behaviour of the three
honoured poets—Longfellow, Emerson, and Holmes—in the log-cabin of
a California miner, about fifteen
years before the date of his speech.
As Clemens represented the case, he
himself, having reached this cabin at
nightfall, sought its hospitality, and
was very reluctantly admitted by the

* *Acts and Anecdotes of Authors.*

occupant, who informed him that the three New England gentlemen just named had spent the previous night with him, that they were much the worse for liquor, passed many hours in card-playing and drinking and quoting poetry, drew revolvers and bowie-knives upon each other, and, on departing, carried off the miner's only pair of boots.

The joke was not very well received, and Mr. Clemens wrote a note of apology, in which he intimated, in palliation of the case, that God made him a fool, and he was simply acting out his nature.

In this connection might be mentioned a dinner which took place at the Parker House, Boston, during Dickens' 1868 tour in the United States, at which, amongst others, " David Copperfield," " Hyperion," "Hosea Biglow," the " Autocrat," and the " Bad Boy " were present.

One who lived through it to tell the tale says : " We had no set speeches at the table, for we had voted eloquence a bore before we sat down . . . We had a great good time . . . Dickens was in his best mood . . . And we all declared, when we bade him good night, that none of us had ever enjoyed a festival more."

There are extremes, after all—the ridiculous and the sublime—which do not meet, as extremes sometimes do, in this mutual - admiration matter. Thoreau once said : " The stars and I belong to a mutual-admiration society;" and he undoubtedly felt there was some hidden and supreme wisdom in what he was saying. The ridiculous was of a certainty present when Madame de Staël and another famous author met by special invitation at a French country house, and each brought a handsomely bound book of her own to present to the other. Both were profuse in their flattery, both declared the other's work would have a priceless value, to be preserved by them with infinite care. When they had made their gushing adieus and departed, the amused hostess found the respective volumes carelessly left on table and sofa. What a subject for the scathing satire of some contemporary wit ! At the time (long ago now, thank Heaven !) of the " You scratch my back, and I'll scratch yours " (was it log-rolling ?), which was carried on in an extremely ridiculous manner between Hayley and Anna Seward, some rhymester penned this sweet dialogue between the interesting parties :

"'Tuneful poet ! Britain's glory,
    Mr. Hayley, that is you——'
'Ma'am, you carry all before you,
    Trust me, Lichfield Swan, you do ——'

> "'Ode, didactick, epick, sonnet,
>   Mr. Hayley, you're divine——'
> 'Ma'am, I'll take my oath upon it,
>   You alone are all the Nine !'"

The cure of such flattery and humbug is sometimes brought about in a rather decided, if harsh, manner. Occasionally a man is found gifted with an unenviable desire to tell the truth at all times, in season and out ; and the awakening is generally brought about by his means. I wonder what degree of positive hatred Sterne felt towards Garrick after the following delightful little conversation between them ! Sterne used his wife very ill. One day he was talking to Garrick in a fine sentimental manner in praise of conjugal love and fidelity.

" The husband," said Sterne, " who behaves unkindly to his wife deserves to have his house burned over his head."

Garrick's rejoinder was simply:

" If you think so, I hope *your* house is insured."

" For it must needs be that offences come ; but woe to that man by whom the offence cometh !"

IV.

SOLITUDE AND SOCIETY; AND THE DEBATABLE LAND BETWEEN.

"But when an eager listener, stealing behind Irving and Halleck at an evening party, found them talking of —— shoe-leather ! and a breathless devotee of Thackeray, sitting opposite to him at the dinner-table, saw those Delphian lips unclosed only to utter the words, ' Another potato, if you please !'—they had revelations which might cast a dreadful suspicion over the nature of the whole tribe of authors.

"I would not have the reader imagine that the members of the Echo Club are represented by either of these extremes. They are authors, of different ages and very unequal places in public estimation. It would never occur to them to seat themselves on self-constructed pyramids, and speak as if The Ages were listening ; yet, like their brethren of all lands and all times, the staple of their talk is literature."— BAYARD TAYLOR.

THE hunger of a great and self-sufficing mind for the charms of re-

tirement is sometimes pathetic in the
extreme. We do not refer here to
that romantic longing of poetic boy-
hood, such as we find expressed
by Kirke White in one of his
sonnets :

"Give me a cottage on some Cambrian wild,
    Where, far from cities, I may spend my days:
And by the beauties of the scene beguiled,
    May pity man's pursuits, and shun his ways.
While on the rock I mark the browsing goat,
    List to the mountain torrent's distant noise,
Or the hoarse bittern's solitary note,
    I shall not want the world's delusive joys ;
But, with my little scrip, my book, my lyre,
    Shall think my lot complete, nor covet more ;
And when with time shall wane the vital fire,
    I'll raise my pillow on the desert shore,
And lay me down to rest where the wild wave
Shall make sweet music o'er my lonely grave."

This is all, without doubt, very
pretty and extremely touching ; but
is it healthy? Although Keats was
mawkish after a manner, his criticism
of life was sometimes remarkably
true, if not very severe. " The imagination of a boy," he writes in his
preface to *Endymion,* " is healthy,

7

and the mature imagination of a man is healthy ; but there is a space of life between in which the soul is in a ferment, the character undecided, the way of life uncertain, the ambition thick-sighted : thence proceeds mawkishness and all the thousand bitters."

The reality which dogs the footsteps of excessive and too far-reaching fancy is sometimes as utterly cruel and ridiculous as that we find pictured in a certain Sequel to Rogers' little poem, *The Wish*, which, in a frolicsome moment, some sportive brain caused to dance into existence,* and which is so complete in its way that we are constrained to give it here :

THE WISH.   (*By Rogers.*)

" Mine be a cot beside a hill,
  A beehive's hum shall soothe my ear ;
A willowy brook that turns the mill
  With many a fall shall linger there.

---

* See *Athenæum*, April 14, 1888.

" The swallow oft beneath the thatch
    Shall twitter from her clay-built nest ;
Oft shall the pilgrim lift the latch
    And share my meals, a welcome guest.

" Around the ivied porch shall stray
    Each fragrant flower that sips the dew,
And Lucy at her wheel shall sing
    In russet gown and apron blue.

" The village church among the trees,
    Where first our marriage vows were given,
With merry peals shall swell the breeze,
    And point with taper spire to heaven."

THE WISH ENJOYED. (*The Sequel.*)

" So damp my cot beside the hill
    The bees have ceased to soothe my ear ;
The willowy brook that turns the mill
    Is turned to please the miller near.

" The swallow housed beneath the thatch
    Bedaubs my window from her nest ;
Instead of pilgrims at my latch,
    Beggars and thieves disturb my rest.

" From out the ivy at my door
    Earwigs and snails are always crawling ;
Lucy now spins and sings no more,
    Because the hungry brats are squalling.

" To village church with priestly pride
    In vain the pointing spire is given ;
Lucy with Wesley for her guide
    Has found a shorter road to heaven."

The shallow sentiment of seclusion
is very different to the knowledge on
the part of great thinkers of the ab-

solute worth of solitude and rest as aids to their life-work. There is nothing, for instance, of "life's young dream" about the utterances of Carlyle on this subject, which we find in his correspondence with Emerson. "Pain and poverty," he writes, "are not wholesome ; but praise and flattery along with them are poison. God deliver us from that ; it carries madness in the very breath of it ! On the whole, I say to myself, what thing is there so good as *rest ?*" And again : "The velocity of all things, of the very word you hear on the streets, is at railway rate ; joy itself is unenjoyable, to be avoided like pain ; there is no wish one has so pressing as for quiet. Ah me ! I often swear I will be *buried* at least in free breezy Scotland, out of this insane hubbub, where Fate tethers me in life." "Solitude," he continues in another letter, "is what

I long and pray for. In the babble
of men my own soul goes all to
babble. . . . My trust in Heaven
is, I shall yet get away 'to some
cottage by the seashore;' far enough
from all the mad and mad-making
things that dance round me here,
which I shall then look on only as
a theatrical phantasmagory, with an
eye only to the *meaning* that lies
hidden in it." "A thinker, I take it,
in the long-run" (Carlyle again to
Emerson) "finds that essentially he
must ever be and continue *alone—
alone:* 'silent, rest over him the stars,
and under him the graves !' The
clatter of the world, be it a friendly,
be it a hostile world, shall not inter-
meddle with him much."

And yet a man of genius, with
sensitive and passionate heart and
powerful imagination (and the possession of these gifts is one of the
hall-marks of genius), cannot find

rest in solitude if he be divorced thereby from his work. The value of solitude to him is that of conditions : unfavourable interruptions are prevented, and his brain-throb goes on healthily and with immediate satisfaction to himself and ultimate satisfaction to the world—if he have it for an audience as a man of superior parts should.

I know of no more charming picture than that of the quiet life of Hawthorne at the Old Manse in Concord, where restful days hemmed him round, and where solitude gave him ample opportunities for literary work. And when a chance friend came to break in upon his seclusion, what a friend that would be ! Emerson* or Thoreau, or, to use Haw-

* "Mr. Emerson delights in him," said Mrs. Hawthorne ; "he talks to him all the time, and Mr. Hawthorne looks answers. He seems to fascinate Emerson. Whenever he comes to see him he takes him away, so that no one may interrupt him in his close and dead-set attack upon his ear."

thorne's own words, "it might be
that Ellery Channing came up the
avenue to join me in a fishing excursion on the river. Strange and happy
times were those, when we cast aside
all irksome forms and strait-laced
habitudes, and delivered ourselves up
to the free air, to live like the Indians
or any less conventional race during
one bright semicircle of the sun."*

* A true disciple of Emerson, or rather, perhaps,
a sharer of some of his thoughts, Hawthorne
saw with him that many a so-called calamity
"commonly operates revolutions in our way of
life, terminates an epoch of infancy or of youth
which was waiting to be closed, breaks up a wonted
occupation, or a household, or style of living, and
allows the formation of new ones more friendly to
the growth of character . . . permits or constrains
the formation of new acquaintances, and the reception of new influences that prove of the first
importance to the next years; and the man or
woman who would have remained a sunny garden
flower, with no room for its roots and too much
sunshine for its head, by the falling of the walls
and the neglect of the gardener, is made the
banian of the forest, yielding shade and fruit to
wide neighbourhoods of men." And seeing this,
he thus wrote with reference to his appointment as
Surveyor of the Port of Salem: "I took it in
good part, at the hands of Providence, that I was

J. T. Fields, in his *Yesterdays with Authors*, gives a very interesting account of a conversation with Hawthorne, which certainly cannot fail

---

thrown into a position so little akin to my past habits, and set myself seriously to gather whatever profit was at hand. After my fellowship of toil and impracticable schemes with the dreamy brethren at Brook Farm; after living for three years within the subtle influence of an intellect like Emerson's ; after those wild, free days on the Assabeth, indulging fantastic speculations, beside our fire of fallen boughs, with Ellery Channing ; after talking with Thoreau about pine-trees and Indian relics, in his hermitage at Walden ; after growing fastidious by sympathy with the classic refinement of Hillard's culture ; after becoming imbued with poetic sentiment at Longfellow's hearth-stone, it was time, at length, that I should exercise other functions of my nature, and nourish myself with food for which I had hitherto had little appetite. Even the old inspector was desirable, as a change of diet, to a man who had known Alcott. I looked upon it as an evidence, in some measure, of a system naturally well balanced, and lacking no essential part of a thorough organization, that with such associates to remember, I could mingle at once with men of altogether different qualities, and never murmur at the change."

And it was Mrs. Hawthorne's perception of the truth underlying the statement that " the changes which break up at short intervals the prosperity of

to interest all who delight to know
of the personality of the author of
The Scarlet Letter. " As the sunset
deepened and we sat together,"
writes Fields, " Hawthorne began to
talk in an autobiographical vein, and
gave us the story of his early life.
. . . He said at an early age he
accompanied his mother and sister
to the township in Maine which his
grandfather had purchased. That,
he continued, was the happiest period
of his life, and it lasted through
several years, when he was sent to
school in Salem. ' I lived in Maine,'
he said, ' like a bird of the air, so perfect was the freedom I enjoyed. But

---

men are advertisements of a nature whose law is
growth," which prompted her, when her husband
brought her the news of his discharge from the
Custom House, to exclaim : " Oh, then you can now
write your book." Hawthorne had been bemoan-
ing himself, for some time back, at not having
leisure to write down a story that had long been
weighing on his mind—the story which ultimately
took shape as *The Scarlet Letter.*

it was there I first got my cursed habits of solitude.'* During the moonlight nights of winter he would skate until midnight all alone upon Sebago Lake, with the deep shadows of the icy hills on either hand. When he found himself far away from his home, and weary with the exertion of skating, he would sometimes take

* " The self-contained purpose of Hawthorne," writes Higginson in one of his *Short Studies of American Authors*, "the large resources, the waiting power—these seem to the imagination to imply an ample basis of physical life ; and certainly his stately and noble port is inseparable, in my memory, from these characteristics. Vivid as this impression is, I yet saw him but twice, and never spoke to him. I first met him on a summer morn- ing, in Concord, as he was walking along the road near the Old Manse, with his wife by his side, and a noble-looking baby-boy in a little waggon which the father was pushing. I remember him as tall, firm, and strong in bearing ; . . . when I passed, Hawthorne lifted upon me his great gray eyes, with a look too keen to seem indifferent, too shy to be sympathetic—and that was all. . . . Again, I met Hawthorne at one of the sessions of a short- lived literary club ; and I recall the imperturbable dignity and patience with which he sat through a vexatious discussion, whose details seemed as much dwarfed by his presence as if he had been a statue of Olympian Zeus."

refuge in a log-cabin, where half a tree would be burning on the broad hearth. He would sit in the ample chimney, and look at the stars through the great aperture up which the flames went roaring. 'Ah,' he said, 'how well I recall the summer-days also, when, with my gun, I roamed at will through the woods of Maine. How sad middle-life looks to people of erratic temperaments! Everything is beautiful in youth, for all things are allowed to it then.'"

Francis Jeffrey's love of the seclusion of his home was intense, especially in his later years. Whatever successes attended him in public life, immediately the excitement was at an end his heart turned to his "old familiar friends," his quiet house and his literary occupations. And so in like manner with Washington Irving. In one of his letters he writes:

" Amidst all the splendours of London and Paris, I find my imagination refuses to take fire, and my heart still yearns after dear little Sunnyside."

And in another :

" I long to be back once more at dear little Sunnyside, while I have yet strength and good spirits to enjoy the simple pleasures of the country, and to rally a happy family group once more around me. I grudge every year of absence that rolls by. To-morrow I shall be sixty-two years old. The evening of life is fast drawing over me; still I hope to get back among my friends while there is a little sunshine left."

Sometimes congenial friends invade the solitude, and the heart grows light. And what conversations, forsooth, take place! Think of the right joyous times when Ben Jonson and Drayton used to visit

a certain William Shakespeare at
Stratford-on-Avon, and were hospit-
ably entertained by the writer of
plays. And if it be true that Shakespeare's death was the result of a too
convivial reception given by him to
these two friends—well, we regret
heartily that no record of the bright
sayings that must have leaped from
lip to ear on that occasion has been
preserved. We refuse to think that
their talk even in their cups was as
the talk of other men.*

The anonymous author of a seven-
teenth century poem, *A Preparative*

---

* Shakespeare and Ben Jonson seem to have
been well matched in controversy. In his *Worthies
of England*, Fuller says : "Many were the wit-
combats between him (Shakespeare) and Ben
Jonson, which two I behold like a Spanish great
galleon and an English man-of-war ; Master
Jonson, like the former, was built far higher in
learning ; solid, but slow, in his performances.
Shakespeare, like the English man-of-war, lesser
in bulk, but higher in sailing, could turn with all
tides, tack about, and take advantage of all winds
by the quickness of his wit and invention."

to Studie; or the Virtue of Sack, begins it thus :

> " Fetch me Ben Jonson's Scull and fil't with sack
>   Rich as the same he drank, when the whole
> {   packe ˌₚₑₐₙₙᵢₐ ᵛᵌ˸ᵤ
>   Of jolly Sisters pleg'd and did agree
>   It was no sinne to be as druk as hee ;"

and Herrick writes :

> " Ah, Ben !
> Say how or when
>   Shall we thy guests
> Meet at those lyric feasts
>   Made at the Sun,
> The Dog, the Triple Tun ?
>   Where we such clusters had|
> As made us nobly wild, not mad ;
>   And yet each verse of thine
> Outdid the meal, outdid the frolic wine."

But 'tis to the Mermaid Tavern, where Shakespeare and Raleigh and the remarkable men of their day met to " exercise their wit," that all who love the poets delight to turn. Keats queried in song :

> " Souls of Poets dead and gone,
>   What Elysium have ye known,
>   Happy field or mossy cavern,
>   Choicer than the Mermaid Tavern ?"

But long before Keats no other than Master Francis Beaumont had written to Jonson :

"What things have we seen
Done at the Mermaid ! heard words that have been
So nimble, and so full of subtle flame,
As if that everyone from whence they came
Had meant to put his whole wit in a jest,
And had resolved to live a fool the rest
Of his dull life."

It has been said that Jonson wrote best when "in his cups ;"* and we are half inclined to fancy that some trifle of truth lurks in the statement. Here are his own confessions: "Upon the 20th of May, the king (Heaven reward him !) sent me £100. At that time I often went to the Devil Tavern ; and before I had spent £40 of it, wrote my *Alchymist*. I laid the plot of my *Volpone,* and wrote most of it after a present of ten dozen of Palmsack from my good Lord T——." And again : "The first speech in my

* He was so immoderately fond of canary that his friends used to call him the Canary-Bird.

Cattilina, spoken by Scylla's ghost, was writ after I had parted with my friend at the Devil Tavern : I had drunk well that night, and had brave notions. There is one scene in that play which I think flat. I resolve to drink no more water in my wine." Was the wine the only source of his inspiration ? or was it not rather aided by the brilliant companionship of the frequenters of the tavern who, coming thither, considered themselves " sealed of the tribe of Ben"?

And who would not if he could have listened to the notable conversations which took place at Hawthornden in January, 1619, betwixt Ben Jonson and William Drummond ?* What has been written concerning the revelation of character which must have been dis-

---

* "Then will I dress once more thy faded bower,
    Where Jonson sat in Drummond's classic
    shade."—*Collins.*

played at this time by both of the talkers is interesting in its way, and on no account whatever to be cast lightly aside. Drummond was undoubtedly eager to hear, and full of talk about poets, who, like himself, were writers of sonnets, madrigals, and courtly compliments : Jonson, arrogant and boasting, yet withal of a warm heart and a kindly disposition, leaned more towards gay and high-born personages, for whom his Court Masques were written. And what entertainment fit for the gods there must have been in their allusions to, and estimates of, such men as Raleigh, Sidney, Bacon, Selden, Fletcher, Beaumont, Spenser, and, above all, Shakespeare, concerning whom Jonson wrote : " I loved the man, and do honour his memory (on this side idolatry) as much as any !"

The learning, judgment, love of anecdote, extensive acquaintance

8

with poets, statesmen, and eminent characters brought into display in these talks must have rendered them enjoyable beyond compare. And before the blazing fire at Hawthornden, no doubt Jonson related to his host all the particulars of the convivial reception afforded to Drayton and himself by Shakespeare at his Stratford home just three years before.

It is ever to be lamented that Jonson's account of his journey to Scotland should have been destroyed in the fire which consumed a great quantity of his papers (probably in 1629), and that from Drummond we have to take all that we can know about their quiet evenings. Not that we believe Drummond to have been insincere ; but what a " labour of love " it would be to compare the records of the same conversations from the pens of the two talkers !

Gifford says that at these times Jonson "wore his heart upon his sleeve for daws to peck at it." Perhaps we should find, were Jonson's account get-at-able, that Drummond also did the same; and no interview between literary friends is worth a spider's egg unless it be accompanied by this wearing of the exposed heart. The evil all comes out in the subsequent injudicious tittle-tattle by either of the parties.*

Pope, in one of his conversations with Spence, told him that Cowley's death was brought about in the following manner: His friend, Dean Sprat, was with him on a visit, and "they had been together to see a neighbour of Cowley's, who, according to the fashion of those times, made them too welcome. They did not set out for their walk home till it

---

* See *Notes of Ben Jonson's Conversations with William Drummond of Hawthornden*, issued by the Shakespeare Society, 1842.

was late; and they had drunk so deep that they lay in the fields all night, which proceeding gave Cowley the fever that carried him off." And this was the Cowley who revelled in his retirement from the busy scenes of the world; who had foregone all public employments to follow the inclinations of his own mind, "which in the greatest throng of his former business had still called upon him and represented to him the true delights of solitary studies, of temperate pleasures, and of a moderate revenue, below the malice and flatteries of fortune." All students of literature know his poem, *The Wish*:

> " Well, then, I now do plainly see
> This busy world and I shall ne'er agree;
> The very honey of all earthly joy
> Does of all meats the soonest cloy.
>   And they methinks deserve my pity,
> Who for it can endure the stings,
> The crowd and buzz and murmurings
>   Of this great hive, the city.

" Ah ! yet ere I descend to th' grave,
   May I a small house and large garden have,
   And a few friends, and many books."

Well, he had his wish so far ; and his death came about, not through his "many books," but through his " few friends."

Alas ! Burns' "few friends " had to do with his end too. The tale is thus recorded by Chambers : "Early in the month of January, when his health was in the course of improvement, Burns tarried to a late hour at a jovial party in the Globe Tavern. Before returning home, he unluckily remained for some time in the open air, and, overpowered by the effects of the liquor he had drunk, fell asleep." A fatal chill resulted, and when he reached his house the seeds of rheumatic fever had already taken possession of him.

Perhaps one of the best stories about Hogg, the Ettrick Shepherd, is that related by Lockhart. The Shepherd was invited by Walter Scott to dinner, and he accordingly came dressed precisely as an ordinary herdsman attending cattle to the market. Mrs. Scott, at that time being in a delicate state of health, was reclining on a sofa. The Shepherd, after being presented and making his best bow, forthwith took possession of another sofa placed opposite hers, and immediately stretched himself thereupon at all his length, giving afterwards as his reason, whilst relating the occurrence, that he thought he could not do wrong in copying the lady of the house. His dirty shoes and greasy hands smeared the chintz; but his ignorance was the hedge which fenced in his bliss, and he saw nothing wrong in it. He dined heartily and drank freely. He jested, sang, and told stories. Soon the wine operated, and threw back the flood-gates of his vulgarity. From " Mr. Scott " he got to " Sherra," from " Sherra " to " Scott," from " Scott " to " Walter," from " Walter " to " Wattie," and finished by calling Mrs. Scott " Charlotte," which " fairly convulsed the whole party."

But with it all the Ettrick Shepherd had a good heart at bottom, and his natural feelings found play and proper exercise in his intercourse with men of his own position in life.* His whole soul went out towards his brother in verse, the unfortunate Tannahill, who committed suicide, by drowning, in his

* " Hogg, talking of him as the man, not the poet, was out of his element in society. . . . At home, within his family circle, the Ettrick Shepherd was a different being ; he had the feelings of the husband, the father, and the Christian, and was, besides, without measure, benevolent and hospitable—full of those charities which commend themselves to the heart." — *Angling Reminiscences of the Rivers and Lochs of Scotland*, by T. D. Stoddart.

thirty-sixth year, having fallen into a state of mental derangement resulting from habitual morbid despondency. "Farewell," said Tannahill, as he grasped his hand a little while before his death; "we shall never meet again!"

Many remarkable meetings must have taken place at one time at the Southampton Coffee-house in Chancery Lane; for here Barry Cornwall, Martin Burney, Mudford (editor of the *Courier*), Hazlitt, Charles Wells (author of *Joseph and his Brethren*),* and Mouncey, among others, used to congregate. There certainly must

---

* The interest in Wells' work has lately been revived by Swinburne, who describes it as "perfect in grace and power, tender and exquisite in choice of language, full of a noble and masculine delicacy in feeling and purpose." He attributes the neglect into which it had fallen "to the imbecile caprice of hazard and opinion." "Notwithstanding," he adds, "the truth remains, that the author of *Joseph and his Brethren* will some day have to be acknowledged among the memorable men of the second period in our poetry."

have been a tolerably free-and-easy
style about these gatherings ; for we
find that the members of the circle
were fond of making bets and laying
wagers on any subject which arose
for question, as, for instance, whether
Dr. Johnson's Dictionary was originally published in quarto or folio.
George Kirkpatrick once lost a bet
he had entered into, that Congreve's
play of *The Mourning Bride* was
Shakespeare's.   He paid in punch.

"Wells, Mouncey, and myself,"
relates Hazlitt, "were all that remained one evening.   We had sat
together several hours without being
tired of one another's company. The
conversation turned on the Beauties
of Charles the Second's Court at
Windsor, and from thence to Count
Grammont, their gallant and gay
historian. . . . Wells then spoke of
Lucius Apuleius and his Golden Ass.
. . . The night waned, but our glasses

brightened, enriched with pearls of Grecian story. Our cup-bearer slept in a corner of the room, like another Endymion, in the pale ray of a half-extinguished lamp. . . . Mouncey sat with his hat on, and with a hectic flush on his face, while any hope remained ; but as soon as we rose to go, he darted out of the room as quick as lightning, determined not to be the last that went."

" It was at the Southampton that Hazlitt, Cruikshank, and Hone used to meet, and discuss the subjects for Hone's next squib. I believe that Hazlitt is answerable for some of the outlines of these, and for suggesting to Cruikshank what he thought was the salient point for illustration. The story goes that he was once trying to make himself understood to Cruikshank, when the latter got up, and, dipping his finger in his ale-glass, traced something in beer on the

table. ' Is that what you mean, sir ?'
he asked, and Hazlitt assented."*

Cruikshank's name is also found
associated with those of the staff of
Punch, who used to meet at the
Crown, near Drury Lane Theatre,
one of the London literary resorts.
"These individuals," says the author
of *Lions : Living and Dead*, describing some of the frequenters, " are
Punch's crack men. The tall one
rejoices in the sobriquet of Michael
Angelo Titmarsh, and is the well-
known author of *Jeames's Yellow-Plush
Papers;* he is also a clever draughts-
man, as witness his designs to his
Vanity Fair, and the little ' bits '
with his artistic mark to them (a
pair of spectacles) in *Punch*—it is
Mr. W. M. Thackeray. The other
party is the still more celebrated (?)
author of *Mrs. Caudle's Curtain*

* *Memoirs of Wm. Hazlitt,* by his grandson,
W. Carew-Hazlitt.

Lectures—Mr. Douglas Jerrold. . . .
That tall, stout personage, with the
short curly hair, red round face,
Jewish nose, and burly form, is Mark
Lemon. He is the editor of *Punch*. . . .
The spare, dark gentleman talking
to him is John Leech, who generally
furnishes the large caricature in each
number, and who is the main prop
of *Punch's* pictorial portion."*

* "The year 1864 came, and found our admirable artist still at work as vigorously as ever;
not robust, not rugged, but in seeming good health
and spirits, and fit to live and work for years. To
Punch, for that year, he had contributed eighty
pictures, when, on the 5th of November, appeared
a very amusing cut : An Irishman, dreadfully mal-
treated in a street fight, is taken charge of by his
wife, while a capitally indicated group of the
victor and his friends is seen in the distance, with
two little Irish boys nearer. 'Terence, ye great
ummadawn,' says the wife of his bussum to
the vanquished hero, 'what do yer git into this
Thrubble fur ?' Says the hero in response : 'D'ye
call it Thrubble, now? Why, it's Enjyement.'
It is as good a thing as ever Leech did—as good
a cut as ever was in *Punch*. When he laid his
pencil down beside this drawing, it was never to
take it up again ; and six days before the appearance of the paper in which the cut was published,
he had passed away."

At the literary breakfasts of Samuel Rogers,* as also at those of Monckton Milnes, one was always certain of meeting people worth listening to. The diary of Thomas Moore is full of such entries as these: " May 20th, 1828.—Breakfasted with Rogers." " 22nd. —Breakfasted at Rogers' ; Luttrell and Lady Sarah Lyttleton the party. . . . After breakfast Sydney Smith came in. . . . Smith spoke of Cooper, the American writer, whom he had been lately visiting." " 23rd.—Rogers having told me he was to meet Scott this morning at breakfast with Chantrey, went there early. Found Scott sitting to Chantrey, with Rogers, Coke of Norfolk, and Allan Cunningham assisting." " June 1st.—Breakfasted with Rogers, the Wordsworths and Luttrell."

* "To love literature and to excel in poetical composition were," says Dr. Mackay, referring to Rogers in his *Memorials of a Literary Life*, "unfailing passports to his regard."

Lady Morgan, who also frequented Rogers' breakfasts, is remembered for her hatred of Macaulay, whom she sometimes met there. The sole reason for her dislike was, one may suppose, that two of a trade never agree; for both were brilliant talkers —Lady Morgan, in fact, has usually been considered a rare gossip. It was at one of these morning parties, when Hookham Frere was present, that Coleridge talked for three hours without intermission about poetry; "and so admirably," says Rogers, "that I wish every word he uttered had been written down."

It is said that Milnes' literary breakfasts, although not so sumptuous as those of Rogers, were perfect in their way, and far more sociable and agreeable to those who preferred quiet conversation to crowds. Macaulay and Thackeray were frequent attendants; and it

need hardly be added that, with the
marvellous powers of memory of the
one, and the caustic wit of the other,
these two in themselves were company sufficient, and their conversation more than ordinary mortals are
usually favoured with.

Years ago, when Tennyson spent
a good deal of his time in London, a
little knot of literary friends had a
standing engagement to dine together
once a month ; and the parties were
almost the ideal of unconventional
friendliness. Among the number
were Carlyle, Cunningham, Mill,
Thackeray, Forster, Sterling, Landor,
and Macready. "Here," says Hattie
Tyng Griswold in her *Home-Life of
Great Authors*, "the conversation was
of the best, Carlyle always coming
out strong, and all the rest content
to listen. However, Carlyle, unlike
many great conversers, never mo-
nopolized the conversation. It was

always dialogue and not monologue with him in any mixed company, though he would discourse at length to one or two visitors.

"Tennyson, like many men of letters, loves to talk about his own work, and is very fond of reading his poems to his friends. This is, of course, very delightful to those friends, if the reading be not too prolonged, although he is said to chant in rather a disagreeable manner. He is a great egotist, and does not like to listen to other people when they talk about themselves. We are told that Charles Sumner once paid him a visit, and bored him very much by a long talk upon American affairs, in which Tennyson took no interest. When Sumner finally made a sufficient pause, Tennyson changed the subject by inquiring if his visitor had ever read *The Princess*. Sumner replied that it was one of his favourite poems, whereupon Tennyson handed him the book, and asked him to read. Sumner began, but was soon stopped by Tennyson, who wished to show him how a passage should be read. He went on reading aloud in his high nasal voice, until Sumner grew very weary, but did not dare to move, for fear of being thought un-appreciative. On and on read the poet, page after page, never making a moment's pause, or giving Sumner any chance to escape, until he had read the whole poem. It is said that Sumner never dared pay him another visit. Being a decided egotist him-self, it was painfully hard for the dis-tinguished American to subordinate himself for so long a time, and his friends amused themselves very much at the idea."

One of the most interesting pic-tures at the Dante Rossetti Exhibi-tion held in London after the poet-

9

painter's death, was a sketch of
Tennyson reading *Maud*, which is
now in the possession of Robert
Browning. This little picture was
reproduced in the issue for December,
1883, of *Harper's Magazine;* and in
a charming gossipy article accom-
panying it, Mrs. Thackeray Ritchie
says :

" *Maud* grew out of a remark of
Sir John Simeon's, to whom Tennyson had read the lines,

> " ' O that 'twere possible
> After long grief and pain,'

which lines were, so to speak, the
heart of *Maud*. Sir John said that it
seemed to him as if something were
wanting to explain the story of this
poem, and so by degrees it all grew.
One little story was told me on the
authority of Mr. Henry Sidgwick,
who was perhaps present on that

occasion. Mr. Tennyson was reading the poem to a silent company
assembled in the twilight, and when
he got to the birds in the high hall
garden calling ' Maud, Maud, Maud,'
he stopped short, and asked an
authoress, who happened to be
present, what birds these were. The
authoress, much alarmed, and feeling
that she must speak, and that the
eyes of the whole company were
upon her, faltered out, ' Nightingales,
sir.' ' Pooh,' said Tennyson, ' what
a cockney you are ! Nightingales
don't say " Maud." Rooks do, or
something like it. " Caw, caw, caw,
caw, caw." ' Then he went on reading.

" Reading, is it ? One can hardly
describe it. It is a sort of mystical
incantation, a chant in which every
note rises and falls and reverberates
again. As we sit around the twilight
room at Farringford, with its great

oriel-window looking to the garden, across fields of hyacinth and self-sowed daffodils toward the sea, where the waves wash against the rocks, we seem carried by a tide not unlike the ocean's sound ; it fills the room, it ebbs and flows away ; and when we leave, it is with a strange music in our ears, feeling that we have for the first time, perhaps, heard what we may have read a hundred times before."*

* " In addition to the Sundays ' at home,'" says J. W. Cross in his *Life of George Eliot*, "the Priory doors were open to a small circle of very intimate friends on other days of the week.   Of evening entertainments there were few, I think, after 1870.   I remember some charming little dinners—never exceeding six persons ; and one notable evening when the Poet Laureate read aloud *Maud*, *The Northern Farmer*, and parts of other poems.   It was very interesting on this occa-sion to see the two most widely known representa-tives of contemporary English literature sitting side by side."

We find a genuine touch of hero-worship in the following short account, by Mrs. Gilchrist, of a visit from Tennyson.   " I was sitting," she says, " under the yew-tree yesterday, when Fanny [the maidservant] came to me and put a card into my

"*The House of the Seven Gables* was finished yesterday! Mr. Hawthorne read me the close last evening!" Who could be pitied for sharing the enthusiasm which prompted Mrs. Hawthorne to pen this announcement? "How you will enjoy the book!" she continues—"its depth of wisdom, its high tone, the flowers of Paradise scattered over all the dark places, the sweet wallflower scent of Phœbe's character, the wonderful pathos and charm of old Uncle

---

hand. And whose name do you think was on that card? If I were talking instead of writing, I should make you guess and keep you in suspense a long while; but that is no use in a letter, because you can peep forward. It was 'Mr. Alfred Tennyson.' He looks older than I expected, because, of course, the portraits one was early familiar with have stood still in one's mind as the image to be associated with that great name. But he is, to my thinking, far nobler-looking now—every inch a king; features are massive, eyes very grave and penetrating, hair long, still very dark, and, though getting thin, falls in such a way as to give a peculiar beauty to the mystic head."—*Anne Gilchrist,* by H. H. Gilchrist.

Venner.   I only wish you could have
heard the poet sing his own song, as
I did ; but yet the book needs no
adventitious aid—it makes its own
music, for I read it all over again to
myself yesterday, except the three
last chapters."

Hannah More relates that when
on a visit to the Garricks in 1776,
David Garrick read aloud to Mrs.
Garrick and herself her (Hannah's)
last poem.   "After dinner," she says,
"Garrick read *Sir Eldred* with all
his pathos and all his graces.   I think
I was never so ashamed in my life ;
but he read it so superbly that I
cried like a child.   Only think what
a ridiculous thing — to cry at the
reading of one's own poetry."

But sympathetic listeners are not
always to be obtained, even for productions of undoubted genius.   " A
touching incident connected with

the manuscript of *Paul and Virginia* is recorded by L. Aimé Martin. Madame Necker invited St. Pierre to bring his new story into her salon, and read it, before publication, to a company of distinguished and enlightened auditors. She promised that the judges she would convene to hear him were among those she esteemed the most worthy. Monsieur Necker himself, as a distinguished favour, would be at home on the occasion. Buffon, the Abbé Galiani, Monsieur and Madame Germain, were among the tribunal when St. Pierre appeared and sat down, the manuscript of *Paul and Virginia* open before him. At first he was heard in profound silence ; he went on, and the attention grew languid, the august assembly began to whisper, to yawn, and then to listen no longer. Monsieur de Buffon pulled out his watch and called for his horses ; those

sitting near the door noiselessly
slipped out ; one of the company
was seen in profound slumber ; some
of the ladies wept, but Monsieur
Necker jeered at them, and they,
ashamed of their tears, dared not
confess how interested they had
been. When the reading was finished,
not one word of praise followed it.
Madame Necker criticised the conversations in the book, and spoke of
the tedious and commonplace action
in the story. A shower of iced
water seemed to fall on poor St.
Pierre, who retired from the room in
a state of overwhelming depression.
He felt as if a sentence of death had
been pronounced on his story, and
that *Paul and Virginia* was unworthy
to appear before the public eye."

The sequel, however, is more
pleasing. " But a man of genius—
the painter, Joseph Vernet, who had
not been present at the reading at

Madame Necker's—dropped in one
morning on St. Pierre in his garret,
and revived his almost sinking courage. ' Perhaps monsieur will read
his new story to his friend Vernet ?'
So the author took up his manuscript,
which since the fatal day had been
cast aside, and began to read. As
Vernet listened the charm fell
upon him, and at every page he
uttered an exclamation of delight.
Soon he ceased to praise; he only
wept. When St. Pierre reached that
part of the book which Madame
Necker had found so much fault
with, the author proposed to omit
that portion of the narrative ; but
Vernet would not consent to omit
anything. When the book was
finished, Vernet threw his arms
about St. Pierre, and told him he
had produced a *chef d'œuvre.* ' My
friend,' exclaimed Vernet, ' you are a
great painter, and I dare to promise

you a great reputation!' Fifty
editions, the year *Paul and Virginia*
was published, attested the wise
judgment of Joseph Vernet."*

We all know Longfellow's translation of *The Blind Girl of Castèl Cuillè*,
with its musical refrain,

"The roads should blossom, the roads should
bloom,
So fair a bride shall leave her home ;"

and now, referring as we are to the
reading of their own works by famous
writers, we remember the charming
account given by Louisa Stuart Cos-
tello, in her *Béarn and the Pyrenees*,
of a visit to Jasmin, the author of
the poem, "who is to the south of
France what Burns is to the south
of Scotland, the representative of the
heart of the people—one of those
happy bards who are born with their
mouths full of birds."

"At the entrance of the Prome-
nade du Gravier," says Miss Cos-

* James T. Fields—*Underbrush*.

tello, "is a row of small houses—
some *cafés*, others shops, the indica-
tion of which is a painted cloth
placed across the way, with the
owner's name in bright gold letters,
in the manner of the arcades in the
streets, and their announcements.
One of the most glaring of these was,
we observed, a bright blue flag, bor-
dered with gold, on which, in large
gold letters, appeared the name of
' Jasmin, Coiffeur.' We entered, and
were welcomed by a smiling, dark-
eyed woman, who informed us that
her husband was busy at that moment dressing a customer's hair, but
he was desirous to receive us, and
begged we would walk into his parlour at the back of the shop.

    *   *   *   *   *

" She exhibited to us a laurel
crown of gold, of delicate workman-
ship, sent from the city of Clemence
Isaure, Toulouse, to the poet, who

will probably one day take his place in the *capitoul*. Next came a golden cup, with an inscription in his honour, given by the citizens of Auch ; a gold watch, chain and seals, sent by the King, Louis Philippe ; an emerald ring, worn and presented by the lamented Duke of Orleans ; a pearl pin, by the graceful Duchess, who, on the poet's visit to Paris, accompanied by his son, received him in the words he puts into the mouth of Henri Quatre :

> "' *Brabes Gascous !*
> *A moun amou per bous aou dibes creyre ;*
> *Benès ! benès ! ey plazè de bous beyre :*
> *Aproucha bous !'*

a fine service of linen, the offering of the town of Pau, after its citizens had given *fêtes* in his honour and loaded him with caresses and praises; and nicknacks and jewels of all descriptions offered to him by lady-ambassadresses and great lords, English 'misses' and 'miladis,' and

French and foreigners of all nations who did or who did not understand Gascon.

" All this, though startling, was not convincing. Jasmin, the barber, might only be a fashion, a *furore*, a caprice, after all; and it was evident that he knew how to get up a scene well. When we had become nearly tired of looking over these tributes to his genius, the door opened, and the poet himself appeared. His manner was free and unembarrassed, well-bred and lively; he received our compliments naturally, and like one accustomed to homage; said he was ill, and unfortunately too hoarse to read anything to us, or should have been delighted to do so. He spoke with a broad Gascon accent, and very rapidly and eloquently; ran over the story of his successes, told us that his grandfather had been a beggar, and all his family very poor; that he

was now as rich as he wished to be ;
his son placed in a good position at
Nantes ; then showed us his son's
picture, and spoke of his disposition,
to which his brisk little wife added
that, though no fool, he had not his
father's genius, to which truth Jasmin
assented as a matter of course. I
told him of having seen mention
made of him in an English review,
which he said had been sent him by
Lord Durham, who had paid him a
visit; and I then spoke of *Me cal
mouri* as known to me. This was
enough to make him forget his
hoarseness and every other evil; it
would never do for me to imagine
that that little song was his best
composition ; it was merely his first ;
he must try to read to me a little of
L'Abuglo—a few verses of *Fronçouneto*. 'You will be charmed,' said
he; 'but if I were well, and you
would give me the pleasure of your

company for some time, if you were
not merely running through Agen, I
would kill you with weeping — I
would make you die with distress for
my poor Margarido — my pretty
Fronçouneto !'

" He caught up two copies of his
book from a pile lying on the table,
and, making us sit close to him, he
pointed out the French translation
on one side, which he told us to
follow while he read in Gascon. He
began in a rich, soft voice, and as he
advanced, the surprise of Hamlet on
hearing the player-king recite the
disasters of Hecuba was but a type
of ours, to find ourselves carried
away by the spell of his enthusiasm.
His eyes swam in tears ; he became
pale and red, he trembled, he re-
covered himself; his face was now
joyous, now exulting, gay, jocose ; in
fact, he was twenty actors in one ; he
rang the changes from Rachel to

Bouffé ; and he finished by delighting us, besides beguiling us of our tears and overwhelming us with astonishment.

" He would have been a treasure on the stage, for he is still, though his first youth is passed, remarkably good-looking and striking ; with black sparkling eyes of intense expression ; a fine ruddy complexion ; a countenance of wondrous mobility ; a good figure, and action full of fire and grace ; he has handsome hands, which he uses with infinite effect ; and, on the whole, he is the best actor of the kind I ever saw. I could now quite understand what a troubadour or *jongleur* might be, and I look upon Jasmin as a revived specimen of that extinct race. Such as he is might have been Gaucelm Faidit, of Avignon, the friend of Cœur de Lion, who lamented the death of the hero in such moving strains ; such might

have been Bernard de Ventadour,
who sang the praises of Queen
Elinore's beauty; such Geoffrey Rudel
of Blaye, on his own Garonne;
such the wild Vidal; certain it is,
that none of these troubadours of old
could more move, by their singing or
reciting, than Jasmin, in whom all
their long-smothered fire and tra-
ditional magic seems re-illumined.

" We found we had stayed hours
instead of minutes with the poet ;
but he would not hear of any apology
—only regretted that his voice was
so out of tune in consequence of a
violent cold, under which he was
really labouring, and hoped to see us
again. He told us our countrywomen
of Pau had laden him with kindness
and attention, and spoke with such
enthusiasm of the beauty of certain
' misses,' that I feared his little wife
would feel somewhat piqued ; but, on
the contrary, she stood by smiling

10

and happy, and enjoying the stories of his triumphs. I remarked that he had restored the poetry of the troubadours ; asked him if he knew their songs ; and said he was worthy to stand at their head. ' I am indeed a troubadour,' said he with energy; ' but I am far beyond them all ; they were but beginners ; they never composed a poem like my *Fronçouneto !* there are no poets in France now— there cannot be ; the language does not admit of it ; where is the fire, the spirit, the expression, the tenderness, the force of the Gascon? French is but the ladder to reach the first floor of Gascon—how can you get up to a height except by a ladder ?"

By a not unnatural transition our attention is carried from this poetic hair-dresser to the baker of Nismes. " In Nismes," writes Hans Christian Andersen, in his *Story of my Life,* "lives the baker Reboul, who writes the most delightful poems; whoever knows him not for this, knows him probably from Lamartine's *Travels to the East.* I found the house, went into the bakehouse, and addressed myself to a man in his shirt-sleeves, who was just putting bread into the oven ; it was Reboul himself ; a noble countenance, expressing a manly character, greeted me. When I mentioned my name, he was polite enough to say that he knew it from the *Revue de Paris,* and requested me to visit him in the afternoon, for he should then be able to receive me better. When I came again, I found him in an almost elegant little room, which was adorned with pictures, statues, and books, the latter not only of French literature, but also translations of the Greek classics. A picture on the wall represented his most celebrated poem, *The Dying*

10—2

Child. From Marmier's *Chansons du Nord*, he knew that I had treated the same subject, and I told him that it had its origin in my schooldays. If I had seen him in the morning as the industrious baker, now he was altogether the poet ; he spoke in an animated way of the literature of his country, and expressed his wish to see the North, the scenery and intellect of which seemed to interest him. With great esteem I took leave of a man to whom the Muses have granted no small share of endowment, but who, however, has common-sense enough, despite the homage which is paid him, to continue at his honest employment, and prefers to be the remarkable baker at Nismes, instead of losing himself in Paris, after a short homage, among hundreds of poets."

We are wondering just here, whether it was indeed the essentially critical attitude of Dr. Johnson's mind which caused him, on hearing one of his papers in the *Rambler* read, to shake his head and mumble " Too wordy ;" and at another time, when his tragedy of *Irene* was being read, to leave the company, giving as his reason for so doing : " Sir, I thought it had been better." But who ever does complete anything according to his own elevated standard ? And how often when men praise most and speak loudest of the merits of this achievement and the other, the author is conscious of the defects of his work in a measure which will never be understood by any other ! The reason lies in the fact that there

> " Dwells within the soul of every artist
> More than all his efforts can express ;
> And he knows the best remains unuttered ;
> Sighing at what *we* call his success.
>
> " Vainly he may strive ; he may not tell us
> All the sacred mystery of the skies,
> Vainly he may strive ; the deepest beauty
> Cannot be unveiled to mortal eyes.

> "And the more devoutly that he listens,
>   And the holier message that is sent,
> Still the more his soul must struggle vainly,
>   Bowed beneath a noble discontent."*

In his *Autobiography*, Gibbon gives us an interesting glimpse of Voltaire at Lausanne. The historian was, at the time of which he writes, a youth of twenty, and was busy completing his education.

"Before I was recalled from Switzerland," he says, "I had the satisfaction of seeing the most extraordinary man of the age—a poet, an historian, a philosopher, who has filled thirty quartos of prose and verse with his various productions, often excellent, and always entertaining. Need I add the name of Voltaire? After forfeiting, by his own misconduct, the friendship of the first of kings, he retired, at the age of sixty, with a plentiful fortune,

* Miss Procter's *Unexpressed.*

to a free and beautiful country, and resided two winters (1757 and 1758) in the town and neighbourhood of Lausanne. My desire of beholding Voltaire, whom I then rated above his real magnitude, was easily gratified. He received me with civility as an English youth, but I cannot boast of any peculiar notice or distinction—*Virgilium vidi tantum.*

" The ode which he composed on his first arrival on the banks of the Leman Lake, *O Maison d'Aristippe! O Jardin d'Epicure,* etc., had been imparted as a secret to the gentleman by whom I was introduced. He allowed me to read it twice ; I knew it by heart ; and as my discretion was not equal to my memory, the author was soon displeased by the circulation of a copy. In writing this trivial anecdote, I wished to observe whether my memory was

impaired, and I have the comfort of
finding that every line of the poem
is still engraved in fresh and indelible
characters. The highest gratifica-
tion which I derived from Voltaire's
residence at Lausanne was the un-
common circumstance of hearing a
great poet declaim his own productions on the stage. He had formed
a company of ladies and gentlemen,
some of whom were not destitute of
talents. A decent theatre was framed
at Monrepos, a country house at the
end of a suburb; dresses and scenes
were provided at the expense of the
actors; and the author directed the
rehearsals with the zeal and attention
of paternal love. In two successive
winters his tragedies of *Zaire*, *Alzire*,
Zulime, and his sentimental comedy
of the *Enfant Prodigue*, were played
at the theatre of Monrepos. Voltaire represented the characters best
adapted to his years — Lusignan,

Alvarez, Benassar, Euphemon. His declamation was fashioned to the pomp and cadence of the old stage, and he expressed the enthusiasm of poetry rather than the feelings of nature. My ardour, which soon be-came conspicuous, seldom failed of procuring me a ticket. The habits of pleasure fortified my taste for the French theatre, and that taste has, perhaps, abated my idolatry for the gigantic genius of Shakespeare, which is inculcated from our infancy as the first duty of an Englishman. The wit and philosophy of Voltaire, his table and theatre, refined, in a visible degree, the manners of Lausanne; and, however addicted to study, I enjoyed my share of the amusements of society. After the representation of Monrepos, I sometimes supped with the actors."

Referring to the composition of *The Chimes*, Dickens once said to

Lady Blessington: "All my affections
and passions got twined and knotted
up in it, and I became as haggard as
a murderer long before I wrote ' the
end.'" He had undergone, he said,
"as much sorrow and agitation" in
the writing "as if the thing were
real," and when the last page was
written had indulged "in what women
call a good cry." But when it was
all finished, and lay before him in
definite characters, nothing would do
but that he should leave Italy to
read it to the choice friends he
loved, and whose approbation he so
thoroughly enjoyed. Accordingly,
Genoa was left behind, and London
reached in little more than three
weeks; and two days after his arrival
he was "reading his little book to
the choice spirits aforesaid, all assembled for the purpose at Forster's
house. There they are," says Frank
T. Marzials, in his charming mono-

graph on Dickens; "they live for us
still in Maclise's drawing, though
Time has plied his scythe among
them so effectually during the forty-
two years since flown, that each has
passed into the silent land. There
they sit—Carlyle,* not the shaggy
Scotch terrier with the melancholy
eyes that we were wont to see in his
later days, but close-shaven and alert;
and swift-witted Douglas Jerrold;
and Laman Blanchard, whose name
goes darkling in the literature of the
last generation ; and Forster himself,
journalist and author of many books;
and the painters Dyce, Maclise, and
Stanfield ; and Byron's friend and
school companion, the clergyman

---

* Carlyle said of Dickens' *public* reading :
"Dickens does it capitally, such as *it* is; acts
better than any Macready in the world ; a whole
tragic, comic, heroic, *theatre* visible, performing
under one *hat*, and keeping us laughing—in a
sorry way, some of us thought—the whole night.
He is a good creature, too, and makes fifty or
sixty pounds by each of these readings."

Harness, who, like Dyce, pays to the story the tribute of his tears."

We are tempted to indulge in yet another picture of a private reading at which Carlyle was present. "Leigh Hunt had invited a few friends with ourselves," says Mrs. Cowden Clarke in her interesting *Recollections of Writers*, "to hear him read his newly-written play of *A Legend of Florence;* and Thomas Carlyle was among these friends. The hushed room, its genial low light—for a single well-shaded lamp close by the reader formed the sole point of illumination—the scarcely-seen faces around, all bent in fixed attention upon the perusing figure, the breath-less presence of so many eager lis-teners, all remains indelibly stationed in the memory, never to be effaced or weakened. It was not surpassed in interest—though strangely contrasted in dazzle and tumult—when the play was brought out at Covent Garden Theatre, and Leigh Hunt was called on to the stage at its conclusion to receive the homage of a public who had long known him through his delightful writings, and now caught at this opportunity to let him feel and see and hear their admiration of those past works, as well as of his present poetical play."

V.

SOCIAL AND IMAGINARY.

" Patchwork may be of two distinct kinds. We may have beautiful and artistic patchwork, made up of brocades, silks, satins, fine needlework, and artistic tapestry; or we may have coarse and trumpery patchwork composed of tawdry and vulgar prints or bits of flaunting handkerchiefs."

" Folk say, a wizard to a northern king
At Christmas-tide such wondrous things did show,
That through one window men beheld the spring,
And through another saw the summer glow,
And through a third the fruited vines a-row,
While still, unheard, but in its wonted way,
Piped the drear wind of that December day."
WILLIAM MORRIS : "The Earthly Paradise."

WHAT evenings in Arcadia those Wednesdays of Lamb's must have been when Wordsworth, Southey, Leigh Hunt, Barry Cornwall, Hazlitt, Coleridge, Talfourd, and such men of culture and imagination gathered round their host! But the "gentle Elia" has been so deservedly written about of late, and every incident in his blameless life has been so read and re-read and dwelt upon lovingly, that aught that could be related to serve our purpose would be but a re-cooking of some tender morsel. The writings of those who were on terms of friendship with him abound with such scraps as the following :

"December 5th, 1826.—Spent the evening at Lamb's. When I went in, they (Charles and his sister) were alone, playing at cards together;" and "Friday, July 13th.—Spent the evening at Leigh Hunt's, with the Lambs, Atherstone, Mrs. Shelley, and the Gliddons. Lamb talked admirably about Dryden and some of the older poets, in particular of Davenant's *Gondibert*," etc., etc.*

* P. G. Patmore.

Of Lamb's "At homes," Percy Fitzgerald writes: "To these nights at his house—to the little rooms, hung round with engravings after Hogarth, and Poussin, Raphael, and Titian—every guest looked back with a fond longing. Milton hung on the wall, and from Milton he would read noble passages, actually weeping as he read."

Hazlitt first made Lamb's acquaintance at Godwin's house, where he found Coleridge, Godwin, and Holcroft in a heated controversy as to whether it was better to have man as he was, or as he is to be. "Give me man," suggested Lamb, "as he is *not* to be." It is interesting to know that the last time Hazlitt (who at one time was ambitious to succeed as an artist) took his brush in hand, it was to paint the portrait of Lamb dressed as a Venetian Senator. "The picture represents Lamb as he was about thirty, and it is by far the most pleasing and characteristic resemblance we possess of him as a comparatively young man. The costume was the painter's whim, and must be said to detract from the whole."*

I don't think Lamb could have forgiven the painter this Venetian-Senator draping of his staid person, for he seems to have taken a sardonic pleasure in misbehaving himself in Hazlitt's company whenever the slightest opportunity offered itself. Even at Hazlitt's wedding he was engaged in some mischief; and it must have been mischief of a kind to please the maker mightily, for in a letter to Southey, nearly eight years after the event, he thus refers to it : " I was at Hazlitt's marriage, and had like to have been turned out several times

* *Memoirs of William Hazlitt,* by W. Carew Hazlitt.

II

during the ceremony. Anything awful makes me laugh."

In his *Letters, Conversations, and Recollections of Coleridge,* Allsop says : " The first night I ever spent with Lamb was after a day with Coleridge, when we returned by the same stage ; and from something I had said or done of an unusual kind, I was asked to pass the night with him and his sister. Thus commenced an intimacy which never knew an hour's interruption to the day of his death.

" Lamb asked me what I thought of Coleridge. I spoke as I thought. ' You should have seen him twenty years ago,' said he with one of his sweet smiles; ' when he was with me at the Cat and Salutation in Newgate Market. *Those were* days (or nights), but they were marked with a white stone. Such were his extraordinary powers, that when it was time for him to go and be married, the landlord entreated his stay, and offered him free quarters if he would only talk.' "

Lamb never ceased thinking and talking of these " Old Salutation " nights with their " egg-flip and Oronooko." There Coleridge and he used to sup occasionally, and remain long after they had " heard the chimes at midnight." " There they discoursed of Bowles, who was the god of Coleridge's poetical idolatry, and of Burns and Cowper, who, of recent poets, in that season of comparative barrenness had made the deepest impression on Lamb. There Coleridge talked of ' Fate, free-will, fore-knowledge absolute,' to one who desired ' to find no end ' of the golden maze ; and there he recited his early poems with that deep sweetness of intonation which sunk into the heart of his hearer. To these meetings Lamb was accustomed at all periods

of his life to revert, as the season
when his finer intellects were
quickened into action.   Shortly after
they had terminated, with Coleridge's
departure from London, he thus recalled them in one of his letters :
' When I read in your little volume
the effusion you call *The Sigh*, I
think I hear you again. I imagine
to myself the little smoky room at
the Cat and Salutation, where we sat
together through the winter nights
beguiling the cares of life with poetry.'
This was early in 1796 ; and in 1818,
when dedicating his works, then first
collected, to his earliest friend, he
thus spoke of the same meetings :
' Some of the sonnets, which shall be
carelessly turned over by the general
reader, may happily awaken in you
remembrances which I should be
sorry to doubt are totally extinct—
the " memory of summer days and of
delightful years," even so far back as

those old suppers at our old inn—
when life was fresh, and topics ex-
haustless, and you first kindled in
me, if not the power, yet the love of
poetry, and beauty, and kindliness.'
And so he talked of these unforgotten
hours in that short interval during
which death divided them."*

In his essay *Of Persons one would
wish to have seen,* Hazlitt says that it
was Lamb who suggested the subject
at one of his pleasant evenings among
friends.

" On the question being started,
Ayrton said, ' I suppose the two
first persons you would choose to see
would be the two greatest names in
English literature, Sir Isaac Newton
and Mr. Locke ?' In this Ayrton, as
usual, reckoned without his host.
Everyone burst out laughing at the
expression of Lamb's face, in which
impatience was restrained by courtesy.

* Talfourd's *Letters of Charles Lamb.*

' Yes, the greatest names,' he stammered out hastily, ' but they were not
persons — not persons.'—' Not persons ?' said Ayrton, looking wise and
foolish at the same time, afraid his
triumph might be premature. ' That is,'
rejoined Lamb, ' not characters, you
know. By Mr. Locke and Sir Isaac
Newton, you mean the *Essay on the
Human Understanding* and the *Prin-
cipia*, which we have to this day.
Beyond their contents there is nothing
personally interesting in the men.
But what we want to see anyone
bodily for, is when there is something
peculiar, striking in the individuals,
more than we can learn from their
writings, and yet are curious to know.
I dare say Locke and Newton were
very like Kneller's portraits of them.
But who could paint Shakespeare ?'
—' Ay,' retorted Ayrton, ' there it is ;
then, I suppose, you would prefer seeing
him and Milton instead !'—' No,' said

Lamb, 'neither. I have seen so much of Shakespeare on the stage and on bookstalls, in frontispieces and on mantelpieces, that I am quite tired of the everlasting repetition ; and as to Milton's face, the impressions that have come down to us of it I do not like; it is too starched and puritanical ; and I should be afraid of losing some of the manna of his poetry in the leaven of his countenance and the precisian's band and gown.'—' I shall guess no more,' said Ayrton. ' Who is it, then, you would like to see " in his habit as he lived," if you had your choice of the whole range of English literature ?' Lamb then named Sir Thomas Browne and Fulke Greville, the friend of Sir Philip Sidney, as the two worthies whom he should feel the greatest pleasure to encounter on the floor of his apartment in their nightgowns and slippers, and to exchange friendly greeting with them. At this Ayrton laughed outright, and conceived Lamb was jesting with him; but as no one followed his example, he thought there might be something in it, and waited for an explanation in a state of whimsical suspense. Lamb then went on as follows: 'The reason why I pitch upon these two authors is, that their writings are riddles, and they themselves the most mysterious of personages. They resemble the soothsayers of old, who dealt in dark hints and doubtful oracles; and I should like to ask them the meaning of what no mortal but themselves, I should suppose, can fathom. There is Dr. Johnson: I have no curiosity, no strange uncertainty about him; he and Boswell together have pretty well let me into the secret of what passed through his mind. He and other writers like him are sufficiently

explicit : my friends whose repose
I should be tempted to disturb (were
it in my power) are implicit, inex-
tricable, inscrutable.'

*   *   *   *   *

" Some one then inquired of Lamb
if we could not see from the window
the Temple walk in which Chaucer
used to take his exercise ; and on his
name being put to the vote, I was
pleased to find that there was a
general sensation in his favour in
all but Ayrton, who said something
about the ruggedness of the metre,
and even objected to the quaintness
of the orthography. I was vexed at
this superficial gloss, pertinaciously
reducing everything to its own trite
level, and asked ' if he did not think
it would be worth while to scan the
eye that had first greeted the Muse
in that dim twilight and early dawn
of English literature ; to see the head
round which the visions of fancy

must have played like gleams of inspiration or sudden glory; to watch those lips that 'lisped in numbers, for the numbers came'—as by a miracle, or as if the dumb should speak. . . .

" His interview with Petrarch is fraught with interest. Yet I would rather have seen Chaucer in company with the author of the *Decameron*, and have heard them exchange their best stories together — the *Squire's Tale* against *The Story of the Falcon*, the *Wife of Bath's Prologue* against the *Adventures of Friar Albert*. How fine to see the high mysterious brow which learning then wore, relieved by the gay, familiar tone of men of the world, and by the courtesies of genius ! Surely, the thoughts and feelings which passed through the minds of these great revivers of learning, these Cadmuses who sowed the teeth of letters, must have

stamped an expression on their features as different from the moderns
as their books, and well worth the
perusal. . . . Lamb put it to me if I
should like to see Spenser as well as
Chaucer, and I answered, without
hesitation, ' No ; for that his beauties were ideal, visionary, not palp-
able or personal, and therefore connected with less curiosity about the
man. His poetry was the essence
of romance, a very halo round the
bright orb of fancy, and the bringing
in the individual might dissolve the
charm. No tones of voice could
come up to the mellifluous cadence
of his verse ; no form but of a winged
angel could vie with the airy shapes .
he has described. He was (to my
apprehension) rather a ' creature of
the element, that lived in the rain-
bow and played in the plighted
clouds,' than an ordinary mortal.
Or if he did appear, I should wish it

to be as a mere vision, like one of
his own pageants, and that he should
pass by unquestioned like a dream or
sound—

————— "' *That* was Arion crown'd !
So went he playing on the wat'ry plain.'

*   *   *   *   *

" We were now at a stand for a
short time, when Fielding was mentioned as a candidate ; only one,
however, seconded the proposition.
' Richardson ?'—' By all means, but
only to look at him through the glass
door of his back shop, hard at work
upon one of his novels (the most extraordinary contrast that ever was
presented between an author and his
works) ; not to let him come behind
his counter, lest he should want you
to turn customer, or to go upstairs
with him, lest he should offer to read
the first manuscript of *Sir Charles
Grandison*, which   was   originally
written in eight-and-twenty volumes
octavo, or get out the letters of his

female correspondents, to prove that
Joseph Andrews was low.

$$* \quad * \quad * \quad * \quad *$$

" Of all persons near our own time,
Garrick's name was received with the
greatest enthusiasm. . . .

" We were interrupted in the hey-
day and mid-career of this fanciful
speculation by a grumbler in the
corner, who declared it was a shame
to make all this rout about a mere
player and farce-writer, to the neglect
and exclusion of the fine old dramatists, the contemporaries and rivals
of Shakespeare. Lamb said he had
anticipated this objection when he
had named the author of *Mustapha*
and *Alaham;* and, out of caprice,
insisted upon keeping him to repre-
sent the set in preference to the wild,
hair-brained enthusiast, Kit Marlowe;
to the sexton of St. Ann's, Webster,
with his melancholy yew-trees and
death's-heads; to Decker, who was

but a garrulous proser; to the voluminous Heywood; and even to
Beaumont and Fletcher, whom we
might offend by complimenting the
wrong author on their joint productions. . . . Ben Jonson divided our
suffrages pretty equally. Some were
afraid he would begin to traduce
Shakespeare, who was not present
to defend himself. . . . At length,
his romantic visit to Drummond of
Hawthornden* was mentioned, and
turned the scale in his favour.

*   *   *   *   *

" By this time it should seem that
some rumour of our whimsical de-
liberation had got wind, and had
disturbed the *irritabile genus* in their
shadowy abodes, for we received
messages from several candidates
that we had just been thinking of.
Gray declined our invitation, though
he had not yet been asked; Gay
offered to come and bring in his

* See p. 112.

hand the Duchess of Bolton, the original Polly; Steele and Addison left their cards as Captain Sentry* and Sir Roger de Coverley; Swift came in and sat down without speaking a word, and quitted the room as abruptly;† Otway and Chatterton were seen lingering on the opposite side of the Styx, but could not muster enough between them to pay Charon his fare; Thomson fell asleep in the boat, and was rowed back again; and Burns sent a low fellow, one John Barleycorn, an old companion of his, who had conducted him to the other world, to say that he had during his lifetime been drawn out of his retirement as a show, only to be made an exciseman of, and that he would rather remain where he was. He desired, however, to shake hands by his representative — the

* A member of the *Spectator* Club.
† See p. 23.

hand, thus held out, was in a burning
fever, and shook prodigiously.

" The morning broke with that
dim, dubious light by which Giotto,
Cimabue, and Ghirlandaio must have
seen to paint their earliest works;
and we parted to meet again and
renew similar topics at night, the
next night, and the night after that,
till that night overspread Europe
which saw no dawn.   The same
event, in truth, broke up our little
congress that broke up the great one.
But that was to meet again : our
deliberations have never been re-
sumed."*

Leigh Hunt's *An Earth upon Heaven*
seems to have been suggested by this
charming essay of Hazlitt's. " Some-
body, a little while ago," Hunt begins,

---

* This paper was written about 1820, but the
event which it purports to describe occurred many
years before.

"wrote an excellent article in the *New Monthly Magazine* on *Persons one would wish to have known* (*sic*). He should write another on 'Persons one could wish to have dined with.' There is Rabelais, and Horace, and the Mermaid roisterers, and Charles Cotton, and Andrew Marvell, and Sir Richard Steele, *cum multis aliis;* and for the colloquial, if not for the festive part, Swift, and Pope, and Dr. Johnson, and Burke, and Horne Tooke. What a pity one cannot dine with them all round ! People are accused of having earthly notions of heaven. As it is difficult to have any other, we may be pardoned for thinking that we could spend a very pretty thousand years in dining and getting acquainted with all the good fellows on record ; and having got used to them, we think we could go very well on, and be content to wait some other thousands for a higher beatitude. Oh, to wear out one of the celestial lives of a triple century's duration, and exquisitely to grow old, in reciprocating dinners and teas with the immortals of old books ! Will Fielding ' leave his card ' in the next world ? Will Berkeley (an angel in a wig and lawn sleeves) come to ask how Utopia gets on ? Will Shakespeare (for the greater the man, the more the good-nature might be expected) know by intuition that one of his readers (knocked up with bliss) is dying to see him at the Angel and Turk's Head, and come lounging with his hands in his doublet-pockets accordingly ?"

VI.

WITH AN OLD LION.

*" And that deep-mouthed Beotian Savage Landor
Has taken for a swan rogue Southey's gander."*
BYRON.

" It was a dream, ah! what is not a dream ?"
LANDOR.

WHILST at Como, Landor received a visit from Southey; and this visit must have been highly gratifying to both if what Landor put into Southey's mouth in the *Imaginary Conversations* was in any way near the truth. "Well do I remember," he makes Southey say, "our long conversation in the silent and solitary church of Sant' Aboudis (surely the coolest spot in Italy), and how

12—2

often I turned my head toward the
open door, fearing lest some pious
passer-by, or some more distant one
in the wood above, pursuing the
pathway that leads to the tower of
Luitprand, should hear the roof echo
with your laughter at the stories you
had collected about the brotherhood
and sisterhood of the place."

The hastiness of Landor's temper
was known to his friends as well
as to himself. Crabb Robinson
speaks of him as a "leonine"
man, with a fierceness of tone well
suited to his name, his decisions
being confident, and on all subjects,
whether of taste or life, unqualified,
each standing for itself, not caring
whether it was in harmony with what
had gone before or would follow from
the same oracular lips.* Robinson

* Landor's conduct in this direction was certainly a brilliant commentary on the words of
Emerson : "A foolish consistency is the hobgoblin
of little minds, adored by little statesmen and

adds : " He was conscious of his own infirmity of temper, and told me he saw few persons, because he could not bear contradictions." And yet between this

"Deep-mouthed Beotian Savage Landor"

and the " Gentle Elia " sympathy of a kind existed.   Whilst in London,

---

philosophers and divines.   With consistency a great soul has simply nothing to do.   He may as well concern himself with his shadow on the wall.   Speak what you think now in hard words, and to-morrow speak what to-morrow thinks in hard words again, though it contradict everything you said to-day."

On the 15th of May, 1833, Emerson dined with Landor, and thus records his experience : " I found him noble and courteous, living in a cloud of pictures at his Villa Gherardesca, a fine house commanding a beautiful landscape.   I had inferred from his books, or magnified from some anecdotes, an impression of Achillean wrath—an untamable petulance.   I do not know whether the imputation were just or not, but certainly on this May day his courtesy veiled that haughty mind, and he was the most patient and gentle of hosts. He . . . talked of Wordsworth, Byron, Massinger, Beaumont and Fletcher.   To be sure, he is decided in his opinions, likes to surprise, and is well content to impress, if possible, his English whim upon the immutable past."

Landor was taken by Robinson to see Charles Lamb, and was delighted with him and his sister. It is said that tipsy or sober, for a few years before his death, Lamb was continually repeating Landor's *Rose Aylmer;* and all admirers of these two famous men must remember the tenderness of the verses addressed by Landor to Mary Lamb on the death of her brother :

" Comfort thee, O thou mourner, yet awhile !
        Again shall Elia's smile
Refresh thy heart, where heart can ache no more.
        What is it we deplore ?

" He leaves behind him, freed from griefs and
        years,
        Far worthier things than tears.
The love of friends without a single foe :
        Unequalled lot below !

" His gentle soul, his genius, these are thine ;
        For these dost thou repine ?
He may have left the lowly walks of men ;
        Left them he has ; what then ?

" Are not his footsteps followed by the eyes
        Of all the good and wise ?
Tho' the warm day is over, yet they seek
        Upon the lofty peak

" Of his pure mind the roseate light that glows
    O'er death's perennial snows.
  Behold him ! from the region of the blest
    He speaks : he bids thee rest."

The decidedness of Landor both in
his likes and dislikes affords us excuse
for referring to two or three other of
his interviews. At Bonn one day he
met Schlegel, and the next the poet
Arndt. Of Schlegel he writes to
Crabb Robinson : " He resembles
a little pot-bellied pony tricked out
with stars, buckles, and ribbons,
looking askance, from his ring and
halter in the market, for an apple
from one, a morsel of bread from
another, a fig of ginger from a
third, and a pat from everybody :"
His interview with Arndt, however,
" settled the bile this coxcomb of the
bazaar had excited." " In one of
the very last pieces of verse Landor
wrote," says Sidney Colvin, " I find
him recalling with pleasure how he
and Arndt had talked together in

Latin thirty years before in the poet's orchard; how they had chanced to hear a song of Arndt's own sung by the people in the town below; and how nimbly the old poet had run and picked up an apple to give his guest, who had kept the pips and planted them in his garden at Fiesole."

In a recent article in the New York *Nation*, we find some interesting particulars of Landor, and from these we extract the following:

"His wife lived in a villa at or near Fiesole for some time, and it was there that, after an absence of thirty years, Landor suddenly rejoined her without a word of notice. He had left her in a fit of caprice, and when he returned as capriciously, he was outraged and indignant to find that no niche in the family circle had been left vacant for him. He had taught his family to do without him, and had left them for thirty years to

practise their lesson, and then was
bitterly disappointed when he found
how well they had learnt that lesson.
Late one night he appeared in
Florence, at the lodgings of his
faithful friends, the Robert Brownings, in a towering rage, and vitu-
perating, no doubt, as only he could
vituperate, against the whole female
sex, and that arch-villain, his wife, in
particular. He would never go back
to her—never! Indeed, it was the
only possible decision to make. He
was at no time an easy man to live
with, and after that little absence
of thirty years, Mrs. Landor may be
forgiven if she did not receive him
with open arms. But she cannot be
forgiven for the long bill which she
sent after him, in which every lemon
that had been made into lemonade
for him during his brief stay was
entered and charged for; and it must
be remembered that the villa itself,

with its garden and all its lemon-
trees, had been paid for out of
Landor's money. Some of the
Florentine courts of justice still,
perhaps, possess records of the suits
brought against Florentine citizens
by this impracticable Englishman.
The last time he appeared, whether
as prosecutor or defendant, in the
Syndic's court, he stooped to hoist
up a heavy bag which he had brought
with him, and which he placed on
the table before him, coolly observing that, as he knew every man in
Florence had his price, here was
money to secure judgment on his
side. The court, feeling itself this
time outraged beyond endurance,
pronounced sentence of banishment
against him, and he left Florence
never to return. Before he was
exiled, Landor had lived in rooms
above those occupied by his friends
the Brownings. They used to send

his dinner up to him every day, and, to a man of his vehement tempera- ment, dinner was a very important event.   He would stand watch in hand when the hour was approach- ing, and if the dinner was a moment behind time, he would seize the dish and hurl its contents out of the window.   Mr. Browning's son, who was then very young, well remembers seeing a leg of mutton pass the window of his father's room on one of these occasions.   An expensive and troublesome inmate, no doubt ; *but what good times the three poets must have had in those long evenings when dinner was forgotten, and there was nothing left to do but talk !*   How they must have enjoyed each other's scholarship !"

I like to think of the pleasure afforded the old lion in his last years by two apparent trifles—the society of a young American lady, Miss

Kate Field, to whom he taught
Latin ; and the visit of Swinburne,
one of his most ardent admirers,
who made a pilgrimage to Florence
on purpose to see the old man's face
before he died.

VII.

BEHIND THE SCENES.

" To say that this taste of ours is a petty taste, the taste of valets, is simply to inveigh against one of the instincts of our nature, the instinct which—to quote the words of Moore—'leads us to contemplate with pleasure a great mind in its undress;' . . . and, perhaps, I may add, to inveigh against one of the strongest charms of history and biography, against the charm without which all history and all biography are little more than 'an old almanack.'"—CHARLES PEBODY.

OCCASIONALLY a poem or work of prose has been the result of some stray hint dropped at a meeting of friends; in other cases, again, the central idea has been the subject of great talk and much beating out before it assumed the importance necessary to prompt its extension into a work of art.

"The account Wordsworth gives of the origin of the *Ancient Mariner* is that in the autumn of 1797 he, with his sister and Coleridge, started from Alfoxden to visit Linton and the Valley of Stones, and their united funds being very small, they agreed to defray the expenses of the tour by writing a poem, to be sent to the *New Monthly Magazine*. Accordingly, as they proceeded along the Quantock Hills, by Watchet, the poem of the *Ancient Mariner* was planned. It was founded, as Mr. Coleridge said, on a dream narrated by a friend of his. Much the greater part of the story was Coleridge's invention, but parts were suggested by Wordsworth ; for example, that some crime was to be committed which should bring upon the ' old navigator,' as Coleridge delighted to call him, the spectral persecution, as a consequence of that crime and his own wanderings."

The origin of Longfellow's *Evangeline* is thus described in the *Atlantic Monthly* : — " Hawthorne, dining one day with Longfellow, brought with him a friend from Salem. After dinner this friend said, 'I have been trying to persuade Hawthorne to write a story based upon a legend of Acadie, and still current there ; the legend of a girl who, in the dispersion of the Acadians, was separated from her lover, and passed her life in waiting and seeking for him, and only found him dying in a hospital, when both were old.' Longfellow wondered that this legend did not strike the fancy of Hawthorne, and said to him, ' If you really have made up your mind not to use it for a story, will you give it to me for

a poem ?'   To this he assented, and
promised not to treat it in prose till
Longfellow had seen what he could
do with it in verse."   What Longfellow did "do with it in verse"
is known tolerably well to the world
now. In November, 1847, Mrs. Hawthorne wrote to a friend : " Have
you seen the most exquisite of
reviews upon *Evangeline*—very short,
but containing all ? *Evangeline* is
certainly the highest production of
Mr. Longfellow."

Burns had a companion whilst
composing *Scots wha hae wi' Wallace
bled ;* but he owed nothing to him
of the kind of debt of either Longfellow or Coleridge. He was indebted to him, however, for his
silence and non-interruption. No
one can tell the story better than
Carlyle ; and so we use what he
relates of the matter : " Why should
we speak," he says, " of *Scots wha hae*

wi' Wallace bled, since all know of it
from the king to the meanest of his
subjects? This dithyrambic was
composed on horseback; in riding
in the middle of tempests, over
the wildest Galloway moor, in company with a Mr. Syme, who, observing the poet's looks, forbore to speak
—judiciously enough; for a man
composing *Bruce's Address* might be
unsafe to trifle with. Doubtless this
stern hymn was singing itself, as he
formed it, through the soul of Burns;
but to the external ear, it should be
sung with the throat of the whirl-
wind. So long as there is warm
blood in the heart of Scotchman or
man, it will move in fierce thrills
under this war-ode; the best, we
believe, that was ever written by any
pen."

Mrs. Hemans relates a conversation she had with Wordsworth in
which reference was made to this

poem. " How much was I amused
yesterday," she says, "by a sudden
burst of indignation in Mr. Wordsworth! We were sitting on a bank
overlooking Rydal Water, and speaking of Burns. I said, ' Mr. Wordsworth, do you not think his war-ode,
Scots wha hae, has been a good
deal overrated, especially by Mr.
Carlyle, who calls it the noblest
lyric in the language?' ' I am delighted to hear you ask that question,' was his reply. ' Overrated !—
trash — stuff — miserable inanity !
without a thought!, without an
image !' etc., etc. Then he recited
the piece in a tone of unutterable
scorn, and concluded with a *da capo*
of ' Wretched stuff !' "

We have a delightful peep into the
inner life of a great writer in George
Eliot's own account of how she came
to write fiction. " One night," she
says, " G. " (Mr. Lewes) " went to

town on purpose to leave me a quiet evening for writing it " (the portion of *Amos Barton* in which Milly's death occurs). " I wrote the chapter from the news brought by the shepherd to Mrs. Hackit, to the moment when Amos is dragged from the bedside, and I read it to G. when he came home. We both cried over it, and then he came up to me and kissed me, saying, ' I think your pathos is better than your fun.' "

Hobbes and Bacon were, it appears, excellent friends, and of great service to each other. Aubrey, in his *Lives of Eminent Persons*, referring to Hobbes, says that Bacon " was wont to have him walk with him in his delicate groves, when he did meditate ; and when a notion darted into his lordship's mind, Mr. Hobbes was presently to write it down, and his lordship was wont to say that he did it better than anyone else about

13—2

him ; for that many times, when he read their notes, he scarce understood what they writ, because they understood it not clearly themselves."

This method of work was altogether out of Goldsmith's line. One day a literary friend was expatiating to him on the advantages of employing an amanuensis, and thus saving time and the trouble of writing.

"How do you manage it?" inquired Goldsmith.

"Why, I walk about the room and dictate to a clever man, who puts down very correctly all that I tell him, so that I have nothing to do more than just to look over the manuscript and then send it to press."

Goldsmith was delighted at the idea, and asked his friend to send his amanuensis the next morning. The scribe accordingly waited upon the doctor, and with pens, ink, and paper placed in order before him, waited to catch the oracle. Goldsmith paced the room with great solemnity several times; but after racking his brain to no purpose, he put his hand into his pocket, and, presenting the amanuensis with a guinea, said:

"It won't do, my friend; I find that my head and hand must go together."

We have so very few genuine peeps behind the scenes upon authors at work, that what Hans Christian Andersen tells us of the elder Dumas cannot fail to prove of interest. He generally found him in bed, even long after mid-day; for it was his custom to have pen, ink and paper in his bedroom, where he wrote his dramas. "On entering his apartment," says Andersen, "I found him thus one day. He nodded kindly to me, and said, 'Sit down a minute. I have just now a visit from my Muse ; she will be going directly.' He wrote on, and after a brief silence shouted '*Vivat !*' sprang out of bed, and said, 'The third act is finished !'"

Sir Joshua Reynolds one day entered Goldsmith's room unnoticed, and found him seated at his desk, with his pen in his hand and with his paper before him ; "but he had turned away from *The Traveller*, and with uplifted hand was looking towards a corner of the room, where a little dog sat with difficulty on his haunches, with imploring eyes. Reynolds looked over the poet's shoulder and read a couplet whose ink was still wet :

"' By sports like these are all their cares beguiled ;
The sports of children satisfy the child.'"

" Surely, my friend," says the genial *Country Parson,* "you will never again read that couplet, so simply and felicitously expressed, without remembering the circumstances in which it was written. Who should know better than Goldsmith what simple pleasures ' satisfy the child ' ?"

The letters of George Eliot to her friends, which have been given to the world in her *Life* by Mr. Cross, show us what a beautifully suitable home-life hers was. " We are delighting ourselves," she says in one of them, " with Ruskin's third volume, which contains some of the finest writing I have read for a long time (among recent books). I read it aloud for an hour or so after dinner ; then we jump to the old dramatists, when Mr. Lewes reads to me as long as his voice will hold out, and after this we wind up the evening with Rymer Jones's *Animal Kingdom*, by which I get a confused knowledge of bran-chiæ and such things—perhaps, on the whole, a little preferable to total

ignorance.　These are our *noctes*—
without *cenæ* for the present—occasionally diversified by very dramatic
singing of Figaro, etc."

Sometimes a meeting of the kind
of which we write is instructive, as
indicating the interest taken by an
old sage in a young, aspiring individual.　Although, in numerous
cases, a man is able to trace the
great and abiding influences which
swoop down upon his life and
overpower it for good, to the printed
pages of some virile author, yet we
often find in actual life that the
influence of man on man, more
especially of man on youth, is incal-
culable.　Now and then, even a stray
thought, uttered in a nonchalant
manner, has immense power over
the future years of the listener.*

* We need hardly say that, in spite of the truth
contained in it, we do not altogether agree with
Douglas Jerrold's saying that nothing is so bene-

It is said that Whittier, the American poet, still dwells upon the singular pleasure he got out of the first sight of his poems printed in the "Poet's Corner" of the county newspaper which belonged to William Lloyd Garrison. That Garrison also found pleasure in them is evident from the following, for which we are indebted to Whittier's biographer, Francis H. Underwood:

"One day, when he was hoeing in the corn-field in the summer of 1826, word came that a carriage had driven up to the house, and that the visitor had inquired for one John Greenleaf Whittier. The youth hastened towards the house in great astonishment, and entered the back-door because he was not presentable, having on neither coat, waistcoat, nor shoes—

---

ficial to a young author as the advice of a man whose judgment stands continually at freezing point.

only a shirt, pantaloons, and straw-
hat. Who could have driven out to
see him ?   After being shod and
apparelled, his heart still in a flutter,
he appeared before the stranger, who
proved to be Garrison. The good
sister Mary, it appeared, had revealed the secret of the authorship
of the poems, and the generous
young editor had come from New-
buryport on a friendly visit.   We
can imagine how the praise affected
the poet ; for the manner and tones
of Garrison were always hearty, and
often very tender, and conveyed
an impression of absolute sincerity.
His position as editor gave weight
also to his words.   To be sure, the
Free Press was a local newspaper,
and in one sense obscure ; but it
was conducted with ability and
conscience, and it reached the best
readers in the county.   For a young
man who had never left his father's

farm this was a recognition unexpected and overwhelming. It was a glimpse of fame.

" The father was called in, and the prospects of the son discussed—the father remonstrating against 'putting notions in his son's head.' With warm words Garrison set forth the capabilities which the early verses indicated, and urged that the youth be sent to some public institution for such a training as his talents demanded. This clear and intelligent counsel made a deep impression, although at first the obstacles seemed insuperable. The father had not the money for the purpose; the farm did not produce more than enough for the necessary expenses of the family. But the son pondered upon the matter, and determined to make every effort to secure a higher and more complete education. A way was opened for him that very year—

not by charity or loan, but by the labour of his own hands. A young man, who worked for the elder Whittier on the farm in summer, used to make ladies' shoes and slippers during the winter. Seeing the desire of young Whittier to earn money for his schooling, he offered to instruct him in the 'mystery.' The youth eagerly accepted the offer, and during the following season he earned enough to pay for a suit of clothes and for his board and tuition for six months."

Whilst in Edinburgh Burns was invited to the house of Dr. Adam Ferguson to meet some celebrated men of letters and science. In one of the rooms he found a picture of a dead soldier in the snow, with his widow and child on one side, and his dog on the other. He was so touched by this picture that he wept. Beneath the print were some lines, and, turn-

ing to the company, he asked whose
they were. No one seemed to know;
but at last a lame boy of sixteen said
they were by Langhorne, and mentioned the poem from which they
were taken. Burns, fixing a look of
half-serious interest on the youth,
said: "You'll be a man yet, sir!"
The boy was Walter Scott, and he
always remembered the incident with
pleasure.

In the spring of 1787 Burns and
Professor Stewart sometimes went
out walking in the morning on the
Braid Hills which overlook Edinburgh. The Professor, speaking of
the poet, says that on these occasions
"he charmed me still more by his
private conversation than he had
ever done in company." Once when
they were admiring the distant pro-
spect, Burns told his companion
"that the sight of so many smoking
cottages gave a pleasure to his mind

which none could understand who
had not witnessed, like himself, the
happiness and the worth they contained."*

Of a surety, as Mr. Strachey says
in his Introduction to the Mermaid
edition of *Beaumont and Fletcher,* " in

---

* Ruskin writes of the Savoyard peasants, in an
altogether different mood, in his *Modern Painters.*
" Is it not," he queries, "strange to reflect, that
hardly an evening passes in London or Paris, but
one of those cottages is painted for the better
amusement of the fair and idle, and shaded with
pasteboard pines by the scene-shifter ; and that
good and kind people—poetically minded—delight
themselves in imagining the happy life led by
peasants who dwell by Alpine fountains, and kneel
to crosses upon peaks of rock ? that nightly we
lay down our gold, to fashion forth simulacra of
peasants, in gay ribands and white bodices, singing
sweet songs, and bowing gracefully to the picturesque crosses ? And all the while the veritable
peasants are kneeling songlessly, to veritable
crosses, in another temper than the kind and fair
audiences deem of, and assuredly with another
kind of answer than is got out of the opera
catastrophe."

" All testifies that (to the Savoyard peasant) the
world is labour and vanity ; that for him neither
flowers bloom, nor birds sing, nor fountains glisten ;
and that his soul hardly differs from the gray cloud
that coils and dies upon his hills, except in having
no fold of it touched by the sunbeams."

the whole range of English literature, search it from Chaucer till to-day, there is no figure more fascinating or more worthy of attention than ' the mysterious double personality ' of Beaumont and Fletcher."

Of the life that Beaumont and Fletcher led in London while work-ing together we know nothing that is positive, and so our imagination has free scope to give them what meet-ings we may in the shape of confer-ences of friendly aid, by suggestion or by absolute work. Speculation, however rife, will never be able to say, whilst pointing its finger at their plays, that this thought or that ex-pression came from the one or the other ; and so we are content to leave it.

Referring to their friendship with another notable writer of plays, Dryden, in his *Essay of Dramatic Poetry*, says : " Beaumont especially being so accurate a judge of plays, Ben Jonson, while he lived, submitted all his writings to his censure, and, 'tis thought, used his judgment in correcting, if not in contriving, all his plots. What value he had for him appears by the verses he wrote to him, and therefore I need speak no further of it." How deep the truth lies in this statement it is difficult to determine nowadays ;* and we are all too busy just at present endeavouring to prove that Bacon was Shakespeare and Shakespeare nobody, to bother about such a minor matter as that of Beaumont instructing Ben Jonson what to put into his plays, and how to put it. We are not, however, too busy to

---

* "Nor is it possible for me to go into the interesting facts which seem to show that it was through a common friendship with Ben Jonson, perhaps through a kindred admiration for the poet's masterpiece, *Volpone*, to which play both contributed commendatory verses, that the comrade poets first became acquainted."—*J. St. Loe Strachey.*

remember that "rare Ben" once shouted "Boo" to a goose!

There is less mystery about the literary partnership of Addison and Steele. The story of their work in the periodicals in which, as Mr. Morley says, the people of England learned to read, is now embedded in our literature. When Steele, on the completion of the last paper of the seventh volume of the *Spectator*, made mention of those who had assisted him in keeping up the spirit of his "long and approved performance," he gave an especial place to Addison, "the gentleman of whose assistance I formerly boasted in the preface and concluding leaf of my *Tatlers*." "I am, indeed," continued Steele, "much more proud of his long-continued friendship than I should be of the fame of being thought the author of any writings which he himself is capable of producing. I remember

14

when I finished *The Tender Husband*
I told him there was nothing I so
ardently wished as that we might
sometime or other publish a work
written by us both, which should bear
the name of *The Monument*, in memory
of our friendship."

What more enduring monument
to their friendship could possibly
have been erected than the seven
volumes of the *Spectator ?*

The tale of the literary partnership
of Mr. Walter Besant and the late
James Rice has been told by the
former in his preface to the library
edition of *Ready-Money Mortiboy.* It
appears that Mr. Besant went to
the office of *Once-a-Week* to secure
remuneration for an article of his
which had appeared in its pages, as
well as to obtain some kind of an
explanation of a number of exasperat-
ing mistakes which had found their
way into it as it stood in print.   Mr.

Besant says he found the editor "a friendly and pleasant creature, anxious to set himself right " with him. This "friendly and pleasant creature " was James Rice, who ultimately joined energies with Mr. Besant; and, as a result, we have that brilliant series of novels with which their names will be lovingly associated for many a year to come.

The story of the authorship of *The Gilded Age*, the joint production of Charles Dudley Warner and " Mark Twain," is thus related : The two men were one day strolling together in the garden of which Warner has written so pleasantly in *My Summer in a Garden*, when Clemens suggested that they should jointly write a burlesque of the popular American novel. It was agreed upon, and the work commenced at once ; but after four chapters had been written, they decided that the subject would not

14—2

admit of such extended treatment, and proposed to make the work a regular story, each writing a chapter alternately, until it was finished.

A hand that has promptly followed a teeming brain, and done good work in literature, can, it need hardly be said, do further good work in the same cause by helping to lift up a struggling brother of the pen to his proper standing-place in the republic of letters. And yet how many have had to bury their good-nature and smother their brotherly feeling at the recollection of the efforts of this kind which have been wasted in the past! In literature, alas! the old story of the ugly duckling is reversed; instead of the much-abused duckling turning out to be the proverbial swan, the would-be swan generally proves to be a little fool of a duck, and a poor thing at that. Of course, there are exceptions, and now and then one

actually does find that the writer who
starts in a heavy, elephantine manner
has, after all, genius of a kind at
bottom, and ultimately does work of
which the world is genuinely proud;
but far oftener our attention is drawn
to a showy dashing character, sparkling with affected Bohemianism, and
of doubtful morals, loose collar, glib
tongue, and self-assumed genius, who
soon gets wiped off the literary record
as a failure and a fraud. Too often,
the fixed star proves to be but a
"farthing rush-light."

If a successful literary man does
seriously wish to turn from his course
and live a life of self-sacrifice, let him
be advertised as of a friendly disposition and willing to teach others
the secret of success in letters. Let
him distribute broadcast scraps of
his autobiography, bristling with tales
(they needn't be too true!) of the
monetary reward of literary produc-

tions—novels, poems (poems especially!), theological treatises (certainly!), heart-confessions, etc., etc.—and his life-work will make rapid descent upon him. He may build barns round about his great estate, window-blinded after the style of lawyers' offices and banks, one blind marked "Poems Religious," another "Poems Sentimental," and so on ; and the manuscripts which shall flood in upon him for his "considerate perusal," "confidential advice," "friendly help in publishing," and "brotherly sympathy and tears," shall so fill his barns that, unless his years have promise of being unduly prolonged to seventy times three-score and ten, he had better insure the premises, set fire to the whole concern, and then, like the foolish man in the Scriptures, arise and build on a more ambitious scale. He should have estimates sent him from manufacturing stationers for the wholesale supply of all kinds of necessary material. Talk about a life of self-denial! that of the veriest pillar-poser of ascetic ages would fade into foolishness and bye-wordism compared with his!

Beware, then, O sane reader, of ever encouraging a man in scribbling! Flee rather for peace to the uncanny wilds of the land of *She*. Many a dabbler in unholy mysteries hath before now raised a throng of devils about him that would not be dispelled, but, hanging on to the last, have even danced upon the unfortunate meddler's corpse.

Yet instances of timely assistance stand out now and then, clean-cut and definite, and laugh to scorn the theories which tend to make a man hesitate before giving his assistance to the multiplying of books, of which there is, verily, no end.

"I received one morning," said Dr. Johnson, whilst speaking of the *Vicar of Wakefield*, "a message from poor Goldsmith, that he was in great distress, and, as it was not in his power to come to me, begging that I would come to him as soon as possible. I sent him a guinea, and promised to come directly. I accordingly went as soon as I was drest, and found that his landlady had arrested him for his rent, at which he was in a violent passion. I perceived that he had already changed my guinea, and had got a bottle of Madeira and a glass before him. I put the cork into the bottle, desired he would be calm, and began to talk to him of the means by which he might be extricated. He then told me that he had a novel ready for the press, which he produced to me. I looked into it, and saw its merit; told the landlady I should soon return, and, having gone to a bookseller, sold it for sixty pounds."

Later on, when in comparatively easy circumstances, Goldsmith used to give dinners to Johnson, Percy, Reynolds, Bickerstaff, and other friends of note, and supper-parties to young folks of both sexes. Blackstone, whose chambers were immediately below Goldsmith's, was at that time studiously occupied on his *Commentaries*, and used to complain of the racket made by his "revelling neighbour."

We all know the story of the first meeting of Thackeray and "Currer Bell," and the annoyance experienced by the lady at the premature announcement that she wasn't a man after all. W. D. Howells has told to an interviewer the following story, which forms a curious parallel, but only inasmuch as it has to do with

another discovery of female personality under manly disguise: " My first
meeting with Miss Murfree (author
of *The Prophet of the Great Smoky
Mountains*) was," he said, " very droll.
She had been writing for the *Atlantic
Monthly* a couple of years.   One day
Osgood dropped in at my library.
' Craddock's in town,' said he ; ' he
will dine with me to-night.   Can't
you join us at dinner?'   I told Osgood
I had an engagement for that night,
but would surely put in an appearance, if only for a few minutes.   You
see, it had never occurred to any of
us that ' Craddock' was not a man,
and I had often given free rein to my
fancy in imagining how he would look
and act.   After Osgood left me he
hunted up Aldrich, and told him
about it, and Aldrich said nothing
but death would prevent him being
present, for if there was one man in
the world he wanted to see it was

Craddock. Then Osgood told Law-
rence Barrett about it, and Barrett
promised to be there too. It so happened that I was the first of the men
to arrive. I saw two strange ladies
in the drawing-room, but no Craddock. Osgood enjoyed my disap-
pointment a moment, and then he
said : ' Mr. Howells, let me present
you to Miss M. N. Murfree, whom
we all know as Charles Egbert Craddock.' The other lady was Miss
Murfree's sister. Of course, I was
greatly surprised, and they all laughed
heartily at my confusion. There was
more laughter when Aldrich came
in, and then we waited to see how
Barrett would take it. I think he
was the most nonplussed man I ever
saw ; he could do nothing for a few
moments but grin—yes, actually grin !
Think of it ! that model of elegance
and dignity grinning ! But he did it,
and he stammered and hesitated so

when he attempted to speak, that the entire party roared until their sides ached."

Dickens, in the Memoir prefixed to Adelaide Procter's *Legends and Lyrics*, relates the following incident :

" Happening one day to dine with an old and dear friend, distinguished in literature as ' Barry Cornwall,' I took with me an early proof of the Christmas number of *Household Words*, entitled *The Seven Poor Travellers*, and remarked, as I laid it on the drawing-room table, that it contained a very pretty poem, written by a certain Miss Berwick. Next day brought me a disclosure that I had so spoken of the poem to the mother of the writer, in the writer's presence ; that I had no such correspondent in existence as Miss Berwick ; and that the name had been assumed by Barry Cornwall's daughter, Miss Adelaide Anne Procter !"

The secret of the authorship of the *Waverley Novels* was well kept by Scott for some time. Procter relates the following instance to show the power of self-command possessed by Scott. It occurred at a breakfast in Haydon's studio. "Charles Lamb and Hazlitt and various other people were there, and the conversation turned on the *vraisemblance* of certain *dramatis personæ* in a modern book. Sir Walter's opinion was asked. ' Well,' replied he, ' they are as true as the personages in *Waverley* and *Guy Mannering* are, I think.' This was long before he had confessed that he was the author of the Scotch novels, and when much curiosity was alive on the subject. I looked very steadily into his face as he spoke, but it did not betray any consciousness or suppressed humour. His command of countenance was perfect."

VIII.

NOT THROUGH INTELLECT ALONE.

" So let me sing of names remembered,
Because they, living not, can ne'er be dead."
WILLIAM MORRIS : "The Earthly Paradise."

SOME remarkable interviews took place between Goethe and Schiller. When they first made each other's personal acquaintance, Schiller was not altogether favourably impressed by Goethe, whose flow of brilliant talk of Italy, travelling, art, and a thousand - and - one other subjects rather oppressed the younger poet. And besides, Schiller's views on some of these topics were out of

sympathy with Goethe's, and yet he
knew not how to contradict him.
Of this interview Schiller writes to
Körner in 1788 : "At last I can tell
you about Goethe, and satisfy your
curiosity. . . . On the whole, I must
say that my great idea of him is not
lessened by this personal acquaintance ; but I doubt whether we shall
ever become intimate. Much that to
me is of great interest he has already
lived through ; he is, less in years
than in experience and self-culture,
so far beyond me, that we can never
meet on the way ; his whole being is
originally different from mine, his
world is not my world, our concep-
tions are radically different. Time
will show."

And time did show, and drew
these two men together by great
bonds of friendship—so great, that
when news of Schiller's death came
to the Goethe household, no one had

heart stout enough to tell it to the master. He, however, suspected something, and said :

"Ah, I see ; Schiller must be very ill."

After a night, in which he was heard weeping bitterly, he arose and said to a friend :

"Is it not true that Schiller was very ill yesterday ?"

For reply he had nothing but sobs.

"He is dead !" murmured Goethe.

"You have said it," was the sobbing answer.

"Dead !" repeated Goethe. "*He is dead !*" and he covered his face with his hands.

Subsequently he confessed to a friend that he felt as if half his existence had been ruthlessly torn from him. His diary at the time was left a blank, the white pages intimating the vacancy of his life.

Years afterwards, whilst on a visit with Eckermann to the pleasant little arbour at Jena, where he and his dead friend used to sit and talk, he said :

" Here it was that Schiller dwelt. In this arbour, upon these benches, which are now almost broken, we have often passed the hours; at this old stone table we have often exchanged many good and great words. He was then in the thirties, I in the forties; both were full of high aspirations, and, indeed, it was something to speak about. Everything passes away ; I am no more what I was; but the old earth remains, and air, water, and land are still the same."

"No two men," said Carlyle, speaking of Goethe and Schiller, "both of exalted genius, could be possessed of more different sorts of excellence. . . . The English reader may form some approximate esti-

15

mate of the contrast by figuring an
interview between Shakespeare and
Milton. How gifted ; how diverse
in their gifts ! The mind of the one
plays calmly, in its capricious and
inimitable graces, over all the pro-
vinces of human interest ; the other
concentrates powers as vast, but far
less various, on a few subjects. The
one is catholic ; the other sectarian.
Goethe is endowed with an all-com-
prehending spirit ; skilled, as if by
personal experience, in all the modes
of human passion and opinion ; therefore tolerant of all, peaceful, collected,
fighting for no class of men or ideas.
Schiller is earnest, devoted ; struggling
with a thousand mighty projects of
improvement ; feeling more intensely
as he feels more narrowly ; rejecting
vehemently, choosing vehemently ;
at war with the one half of things, in
love with the other half ; hence dis-
satisfied, impetuous, without internal

rest, and scarcely conceiving the pos-
sibility of such a state."

For lovers of books I can think
of no more pleasing interview than
that which took place between
Petrarch and Richard de Bury.
Petrarch was not only a poet; he
was a lover of books, and in his way
a great collector. De Bury's book-
loving and book-collecting propen-
sities were very pronounced, as we
all know. What common ground,
then, for conversation! How De
Bury's eyes must have glistened, and
his heart warmed, as Petrarch exhibited his precious manuscripts one
after the other! Petrarch, by the
way, was too good-natured by far;
his books were always at the service
of his friends, and, although some
were returned in due course, others
got astray in a mysterious fashion.
A magnificent manuscript of Cicero's
De Gloria was even pawned by

15—2

one who had borrowed it of the poet.

But 'tis to the friendship which existed between Petrarch and Boccaccio that we turn our broadest human sympathies. Francis Hueffer, in an article entitled *A Literary Friendship of the Fourteenth Century*, gives us a pleasing account of how the inner life of the one was bound to that of the other. They seem both to have had an early experience of failure in things worldly, which really has not been phenomenal with men of genius through the ages. Petrarch was the son of a notary, and Boccaccio of a merchant; and they were both brought up to the fathers' callings. But neither of them showed taste or talent for the practical pursuits of life. Boccaccio's master sent back his idle clerk in despair after six years' apprenticeship, and an equal term spent by

Petrarch in the study of the law was
counted by him as an utter and irre-
trievable loss of time.

Their friendship, when it came
about later in their lives, had nothing
hollow and mocking about it. The
power and purse of each were at the
command of the other to use as he
would. For our present purpose,
however, we must pass the years by
until they bring us to the messenger
Boccaccio, visiting Petrarch with
complimentary offers from Florence
of a chair in the University. " Boccaccio remained with Petrarch,"
says Mr. Hueffer, "for some time,
and the account he has given of his
visit conveys a pleasant idea of the
genial, unceremonious intercourse of
the two friends. Even for such a
guest Petrarch would not interrupt
his studies, and Boccaccio himself
began at once to copy the most important works of his friend, the pos-

session of which had been the goal of his wishes for a long time. But after their work, in the evenings, the two friends used to meet in a little orchard, beautiful with the blossoms of spring, and communicate to each other the ideas nearest and dearest to their hearts."

IX.

CAMPING OUT.

"... the fires of vagabondage which smoulder beneath the surface of most men's conventionalisms—which mountain and river and winds had liberated and fanned.... Deep in our hearts we hide the diminished flame, and brood above it with memories of forest and mere."—J. CHAPMAN WOODS.

WHITTIER gives us an attractive picture in his poem, *The Tent on the Beach*, of three literary friends, who

" When heats as of a tropic clime
    Burned all our inland valleys through,
   *   *   *   *   *

    Pitched their white tents where sea-winds
        blew.
   *   ,   *   *   *

" They rested there, escaped awhile
    From cares that wear the life away,
  To eat the lous of the Nile
    And drink he poppies of Cathay—

To fling their loads of custom down,
Like drift-weed on the sand-slopes brown,
And in the sea-waves drown the restless pack
Of duties, claims, and needs that barked upon their
    track."

These three friends, Whittier, Fields, and Bayard Taylor, have quite a Bohemian time of it, hearing

" The bells of morn and night
Swing, miles away, their silver speech."

Our readers—at least, the few of them who know not Whittier—must go to the poem for the stories; just here the Quaker-poet shall give us only the portraits of the " companions three " :

" One,* with his beard scarce silvered, bore
    A ready credence in his looks,
A lettered magnate, lording o'er
    An ever-widening realm of books.
In him brain-currents, near and far,
    Converged as in a Leyden jar;
The old, dead authors thronged him round about,
And Elzevir's gray ghosts from leathern graves
    looked out.

" Pleasant it was to roam about
    The lettered world as he had done,

And see the lords of song without
 Their singing robes and garlands on :
With Wordsworth paddle Rydal mere,
 Taste rugged Elliott's home-brewed beer,
And with the ears of Rogers at fourscore,
Hear Garrick's buskined tread and Walpole's wit
  once more."

Whittier draws his own picture :

" And one there was a dreamer born,
 Who, with a mission to fulfil,
Had left the Muses' haunts to turn
 The crank of an opinion mill,
Making his rustic reed of song
A weapon in the war with wrong,
Yoking his fancy to the breaking plough
That beam-deep turned the soil for truth to spring
  and grow.

" For while he wrought with strenuous will
 The work his hands had found to do,
He heard the fitful music still
 Of winds that out of dreamland blew.
The din about him could not drown
What the strange voices whispered down ;
Along his task-field weird processions swept,
The visionary pomp of stately phantoms stepped.

" The common air was thick with dreams—
 He told them to the toiling crowd ;
Such music as the woods and streams
 Sang in his ear he sang aloud."

Bayard Taylor was the

" One whose Arab face was tanned
 By tropic sun and boreal frost,
So travelled there was scarce a land
 Or people left him to exhaust,

In idling mood had from him hurled
The poor squeezed orange of the world,
And in the tent-shade, as beneath a palm,
Smoked, cross-legged like a Turk, in Oriental
    calm.

" The very waves that washed the sand
    Below him he had seen before
Whitening the Scandinavian strand
    And sultry Mauritanian shore.
From ice-rimmed isles, from summer seas,
    Palm-fringed, they bore him messages ;
He heard the plaintive Nubian songs again,
And mule-bells tinkling down the mountain-paths
    of Spain."

X.

A PASSING GLIMPSE.

" I yield the palm to no man's love! but others loved thee first."

I WONDER what particular associations were present in the mind of Hawthorne, as he strolled about London with his friend Bennock in search of Johnson's old haunts! Were the worthy doctor's pompous phrases coursing through his mind?* or did he recollect the fact that one

* "A fine day," said Sir Joshua Reynolds to Dr.'Johnson.
"Sir," he answered, "it seems propitious, but the atmosphere is humid and the skies are nebulous."
Any recorded conversations with Johnson always make me think of the interesting question of the languid young lady who wished to ring the tea-

night in particular Savage and Johnson walked round and about St. James's Square for want of a lodging, and were not at all depressed at their situation, but, in high spirits and brimful of patriotism, traversed the square for several hours ? Only a few years after this homeless night, and Johnson stood, a literary Colossus, on the enduring pedestal of fame, and Savage, a murderer and a profligate, ended his miserable career in Bristol gaol.

But Boswell, as leader of all writers on Johnson, has done his work so

---

bell. " If I agitate the communicator," she asked, " will the domestic appear ?"

The following is certainly an excellent imitation of the style of the worthy doctor :

" What is a window ?" asked an earnest seeker after knowledge.

" A window, sir," replied Johnson, " is an orifice cut out of an edifice for the introduction of illumination."

" Thank you; will you be good enough to snuff the candle ?"

" Sir, you ought rather to say, deprive that luminary of its superfluous eminence."

thoroughly that it were folly for us to repeat here any of the well-known stories of the great man which have become embedded in our literature. And, besides, an oak-tree is out of place in the tiny beds of a close-cut lawn. Dwarf plants should be there, with an occasional rose-bush, making bright bits of colour, and filling the air with sweet scents. Let the big tree flourish in some neighbouring field, where it has room to throw out its mighty roots and branches!

Shelley certainly is not one of our oak-trees of literature ; but, thanks to the present revival of interest in him, both as a man and a poet, his personality has become so pronounced that we all know him— some will perhaps have it, even better than he knew himself—and so we linger here but for a moment to bestow on him a passing look of sad farewell. In spirit we bend our heads with Byron, Hunt, and Trelawny* over the body of the dead poet, lying on the Tuscan coast, about to be reduced to ashes. "A furnace was provided, of iron bars and strong sheet-iron, with fuel, and frankincense, wine, salt and oil, the accompaniments of a Grecian cremation : the volume of Keats was burned along with the body. It was a glorious day, and a splendid pros-pect—the cruel and calm sea before, the Apennines behind. A curlew wheeled close to the pyre, screaming, and would not be driven away; the flame arose golden and towering." And so we pass on, with chastened soul and sad heart, leaving Hunt and Byron behind. The world has been robbed of a dreamer !

* " To hear Trelawny speak of Shelley," said Swinburne, "is beautiful and touching ; at that name his voice (usually that of an old sea-king, as he is) always changes and softens unconsciously. 'There,' he said to me, 'was the very best of men, and he was treated as the very worst.' "

XI.

A GIANT IN THE PATH.

"In the centre of all, and object of all, stands the Human Being, towards whose heroic and spiritual evolution poems and everything directly or indirectly tend."—WALT WHITMAN.

THE grim persistency of Carlyle— the dogged determination which enabled him to overcome obstacles which would have taken the life out of most men, appears to have been in a measure characteristic of the Carlyle family. In his *Reminiscences of Carlyle*, Mr. A. J. Symington tells the following story, which will speak for itself:

"While walking in Rotten Row, he (Carlyle) told me how his brother

John, who had been twenty years in Italy, as physician to the Duke of Buccleuch, had amassed an enormous amount of Dante material towards executing a prose translation. For long he had unsuccessfully urged his brother to set about it ; but, urge and progue as he would, he could not get him to begin. So he resolved on trying quite another plan, and bethought him of the man who was driving pigs to Killarney, and who told his friend to hush and speak low, for the pigs thought he wanted them to go the other way. This story he told with great animation, standing still the while, and acting it inimitably, saying, after he had finished : ' *That* is how I got John to begin his translation, and thus it came about. One day said I : " John, man, if I were in your shoes, I would get quit of that Dante business, which hangs about your neck like a dead albatross.

Cast it away from you, and give up all thought of ever translating Dante. If you had been a young man, you might have looked forward to over-taking it; but now you are *too old*. Read and enjoy yourself, and bother your head no more about Dante." '

" The steel struck fire," said Carlyle, " as was intended. John exclaimed : ' Me *too old !* I'm nothing of the kind !' And, so, forthwith, he set to work, and produced one of the very best translations of Dante to be found anywhere."

When Hjalmar Hjorth Boyesen visited Turgenieff in Paris some years ago, they fell talking of Carlyle. Turgenieff related that once he visited the Chelsea sage, and found him loud in his denunciation of democ-racy, and very unreserved in his expression of sympathy with Russia and her Emperor.

" This grand moving of great

16

masses swayed by one powerful hand, brings," he said, "uniformity and purpose into history. In a country like Great Britain, it was wearisome to see how every petty individual could thrust forth his head, like a frog out of its swamp, and croak away at his contemptible sentiment as long as anybody had a mind to listen to him. Such a state of things could only result in confusion and disorder."

Turgenieff told Carlyle in reply that he should only ask him to go to Russia and spend a month or two in one of the interior governments, just long enough to observe with his own eyes the effect of this much-admired despotism. Then, he thought, he would need no word of his to convince him.

One day Carlyle met Browning, and wished to say something pleasant about *The Ring and the Book;* but somehow he got sadly mixed, with the result that what he did say was not entirely a compliment. " It is a wonderful book," he said; "one of the most wonderful poems ever written. I re-read it all through— all made out of an Old Bailey story, that might have been told in ten lines, and only wants forgetting."

XII.

"FOUND AGAIN IN THE HEART OF A FRIEND."

" Perhaps the best of a song heard, or of any and all true love, or life's fairest episodes, or sailors', soldiers' trying scenes on land or sea, is the floating résumé of them, or any of them, long afterwards, looking at the actualities away back past, with all their practical excitations gone. How the soul loves to hover over such reminiscences !"—WALT WHITMAN.

MOST of us know that charming little poem of Longfellow's — *The Arrow and the Song :*

" I shot an arrow into the air,
   It fell to earth I knew not where ;
   For, so swiftly it flew, the sight
   Could not follow it in its flight.

" I breathed a song into the air,
   It fell to earth, I knew not where ;
   For who has sight so keen and strong,
   That it can follow the flight of song ?

" Long, long afterwards, in an oak
I found the arrow, still unbroke ;
And the song from beginning to end,
I found again in the heart of a friend."

What pleasure a man like Wordsworth must have reaped when he
found any of his poetry embedded in
the memory of a friend !

Perhaps one of the most interesting instances of finding one's words
in an unlooked-for quarter is the
following :

" John Howard Payne, the author
of *Home, Sweet Home*, was a warm
personal friend of John Ross, who
will be remembered as the celebrated
chief of the Cherokees. At the time
the Cherokees were removed from
their homes in Georgia to their
present possessions west of the
Mississippi River, Payne was spend-
ing a few weeks in Georgia with
Ross, who was occupying a miserable
cabin, having been forcibly ejected
from his former home. A number

of the prominent Cherokees were in prison, and that portion of Georgia in which the tribe was located was scoured by armed squads of the Georgia militia, who had orders to arrest all who refused to leave the country. While Ross and Payne were seated before the fire in the hut, the door was suddenly burst open and six or eight militiamen sprang into the room. The soldiers lost no time in taking their prisoners away. Ross was permitted to ride his own horse, while Payne was mounted on one led by a soldier. As the little party left the hovel, rain began falling, and continued until every man was drenched thoroughly. The journey lasted all night. Towards midnight, Payne's escort, in order to keep himself awake, began humming *Home, Sweet Home,* when Payne remarked:

" ' Little did I expect to hear that

song under such circumstances, and at such a time. Do you know the author ?'

" ' No,' said the soldier. ' Do you ?"

" ' Yes,' answered Payne ; ' I composed it.'*

" ' The devil you did ! You can tell that to some fellows, but not to me. Look here ; you made that song, you say. If you did—and I know you didn't—you can say it all without stopping. It has something in it about pleasures and palaces. Now, ·pitch in, and reel it off; and if you can't, I'll bounce you from your horse, and lead you instead of it.'

" The threat was answered by

---

* " Payne declared that he had heard the tune of *Home, Sweet Home* from the lips of a Sicilian peasant girl, who sang it artlessly as she sold some sort of Italian wares, and touched his fine ear by the purity of her voice. It is pleasant to think he did not crib it from an old opera, but had a certain proprietorship in the air, as well as the words, of the most popular song extant."

Payne, who repeated the song in a slow, subdued tone, and then sang it, making the old woods ring with the tender melody and pathos of the words. It touched the heart of the rough soldier, who was not only captivated but convinced, and who said the composer of such a song should never go to prison if he could help it. And when the party reached Milledgeville, they were, after a preliminary examination, discharged, much to their surprise. Payne insisted it was because the leader of the squad had been under the magnetic influence of Ross's conversation, and Ross insisted that they had been saved from insult and imprisonment by the power of *Home, Sweet Home*, sung as only those who feel can sing it. The friendship existing between Ross and Payne endured until the grave closed over the mortal remains of the latter."

" On my return home from Paris,"
writes Hans Christian Andersen, in
his *Story of My Life,* " I went along
the Rhine; I knew that in one of the
Rhine towns the poet Freiligrath
lived. The picturesque in his poems
pleased me very much, and I wished
to become acquainted with him. I
stopped in some towns on the Rhine,
and inquired after him ; in St. Goars
I was shown the house where he
lived. He was sitting at his writing-
table, and seemed annoyed at being
disturbed by a stranger. I told not
my name, but only that I could not
pass by St. Goars without paying
my respects to the poet Freiligrath.
' That is very kind of you,' said he,
in a cold tone, and asked who I
was. When I replied : ' We both
have one and the same friend,
Chamisso,' he sprang up in an
ecstasy of joy. ' Andersen !' he exclaimed ; ' it is !' He flung himself

on my neck, and his honest eyes beamed. 'Now stay for some days here,' said he. I told him that I could stay only two hours, as I was in company with countrymen who were waiting for me. 'You have many friends in little St. Goars,' said he. 'I have, a short time since, read out to a great circle your novel of *O. F.* One of these friends, however, I must fetch here, and you must also see my wife. Ay, know you not yet that you have had some share in our marriage?' And now he told how my novel of *Only a Fiddler* had brought them into a correspondence by letter, and, eventually, into an acquaintance, which ended in their becoming a married couple. He called her, told her my name, and I was considered as an old friend."

XIII.

SUNSHINE WHICH NEVER CAME.

" And it passed over our heads on to the haw-thorn-bushes in the field across the brook."

IN a list of interviews which should have taken place I certainly would include one between Tennyson and Landor. The invitation of the latter, which we cannot find was ever accepted, runs thus :

> " I entreat you, Alfred Tennyson,
> Come and share my haunch of venison.
> I have, too, a bin of claret,
> Good, but better when you share it.
> Tho' 'tis only a small bin,
> There's a stock of it within.
> And as sure as I'm a rhymer,
> Half a butt of Rudesheimer.
> Come ; among the sons of men is none
> Welcomer than Alfred Tennyson."

Tennyson and Hawthorne should also have enjoyed each other's spoken word. It was a matter of regret afterwards to both that one opportunity, at least, of so doing was permitted to slip by. Hawthorne thus mentions it: " While I was among the Dutch painters (at the Manchester Exhibition of 1857), —— accosted me. He told me that the ' Poet Laureate ' (as he called him) was in the Exhibition rooms, and, as I expressed great interest, was kind enough to go in quest of him ; not for the purpose of introduction, however, for he was not acquainted with Tennyson. Soon Mr. —— returned, and said he had found the Poet Laureate, and going into the saloon of the Old Masters, we saw him there, in company with Mr. Woolner. . . . Gazing at him with all my eyes, I liked him well, and rejoiced more in him than in all

the wonders of the Exhibition. . . .
I would gladly have seen more of
this one poet of our day, but forbore
to follow him; for I must own that it
seemed mean to be dogging him
through the saloons, or even to look
at him, since it was to be done
stealthily, if at all."

In his *Yesterdays with Authors*, J.
T. Fields refers to this same incident.
" It was," he says, " during one of his
rambles with Alexander Ireland
through the Manchester Exhibition
rooms that Hawthorne saw Tennyson wandering about. I have always
thought it unfortunate that these two
men of genius could not have been
introduced on that occasion. Hawthorne was too shy to seek an introduction, and Tennyson was not aware
that the American author was present.
Hawthorne records in his journal that
he gazed at Tennyson with all his
eyes, ' and rejoiced more in him than

in all the other wonders of the Exhibition.' When I afterwards told Tennyson that the author whose *Twice-told Tales* he happened to be then reading at Farringford had met him at Manchester, but did not make himself known, the Laureate said in his frank and hearty manner : ' Why didn't he come up and let me shake hands with him? I am sure I should have been glad to meet a man like Hawthorne anywhere.' "

When Samuel Rogers, the poet, was a young man in his father's bank, his spirit of hero-worship sug-gested a visit to Dr. Johnson; but, on reaching his house in Bolt Court, his courage forsook him as he was about to lift the knocker.

In still more modern times I would that Robert Buchanan had found his way to Chelsea, and lifted the knocker of a certain house wherein dwelt Dante Gabriel Rossetti. We

all know of the literary quarrel between these two authors, and the
tender verses Buchanan subsequently
penned to the poet-painter, followed
by that other lament after death had
closed his eyes.

What a meeting Hawthorne, with
the delicate kindliness of his nature,
has conjured up for us at the close of
his notice of Delia Bacon, whose
enthusiastic mind got disarranged
over her efforts to dethrone Shakespeare in favour of Bacon, and who
ultimately became hopelessly insane!
"And when, not many months after
the outward failure of her life-long
object," he writes, "she passed into
the better world, I know not why we
should hesitate to believe that the
immortal poet may have met her on
the threshold and led her in, re-
assuring her with friendly and comfortable words, and thanking her
(yet with a smile of gentle humour

in his eyes at the thought of certain
mistaken speculations) for having
interpreted him to mankind so
well."*

---

* In a letter to Mary Cowden Clarke, con-
gratulating her on the completion of her *Con-
cordance to Shakespeare*, Douglas Jerrold writes :
" On your first arrival in Paradise you must expect
a kiss from Shakespeare—even though your husband should *happen* to be there." Some little
time after, in a brilliant article in *Punch*, on " The
Shakespeare Night " at Covent Garden Theatre,
which took place the 7th December, 1847, the
same delightful author, after describing the festive
happiness of the affair, proceeds : " At a few
minutes to seven, and quite unexpectedly, William
Shakespeare, with his wife, the late Anne Hatha-
way, drove up to the private box door, drawn by
Pegasus, for that night only appearing in harness.
. . . Shakespeare was received — and afterwards
lighted to his box—by his editors, Charles Knight
and Payne Collier, upon both of whom the poet
smiled benignly ; and saying some pleasant, com-
mendable words to each, received from their hands
their two editions of his immortality. And then
from a corner Mrs. Cowden Clarke, timidly, and
all one big blush, presented a play-bill, with some
Hesperian fruit (of her own gathering). Shakespeare knew the lady at once ; and taking her
two hands, and looking a Shakespearian look into
her now pale face, said in tones of unimaginable
depth and sweetness, ' But where is *your* book,
Mistress Mary Clarke ? Where is your *Concord-
ance ?*' And, again pressing her hands, with a
smile of sun-lighted Apollo, he said, ' I pray you let

Leigh Hunt liked to sum up in his mind the famous authors who, with hand clasped in hand, completed the chain of genius for generations. It was a subject which charmed him as if he had been a witness to the passing of the mantle of Elijah on to the shoulders of Elisha, or heard the dread secrets which, of old, Archdruid after Archdruid whispered to his chosen successor.

" It is a curious and pleasant thing," says Hunt, " to consider that a link of personal acquaintance can be traced from the authors of our own times to those of Shakespeare, and to Shakespeare himself. Ovid,

---

me take it home with me.' And Mrs. Clarke, having no words, dropped the profoundest ' Yes,' with knocking knees. ' A very fair and cordial gentlewoman, Anne,' said Shakespeare, aside to his wife ; but Anne merely observed that ' It was just like him ; he was always seeing something fair where nobody else saw anything. The woman —odds her life !—was well enough.' And Shakespeare smiled again."

17

in recording his intimacy with Pro-
pertius and Horace, regrets that he
had only seen Virgil (*First,* Lib. iv.,
v. 51). But still he thinks the sight
of him worth remembering. And
Pope, when a child, prevailed on
some friends to take him to a coffee-
house which Dryden frequented,
merely to look at him, which he did
with great satisfaction. Now, such
of us as have shaken hands with a
living poet might be able to reckon
up a series of connecting shakes, to
the very hand that wrote of Hamlet,
and of Falstaff, and of Desdemona.

"With some living poets, it is
certain. There is Thomas Moore,
for instance, who knew Sheridan.
Sheridan knew Johnson, who was
the friend of Savage, who knew
Steele, who knew Pope. Pope was
intimate with Congreve, and Congreve with Dryden. Dryden is said
to have visited Milton. Milton is

said to have known Davenant, and
to have been saved by him from the
revenge of the restored court, in return for having saved Davenant from
the revenge of the Commonwealth.
But if the link between Dryden and
Milton, and Milton and Davenant, is
somewhat apocryphal, or rather de-
pendent on tradition (for Richardson
the painter tells us the story from
Pope, who had it from Betterton the
actor, one of Davenant's company),
it may be carried at once from
Dryden to Davenant, with whom he
was unquestionably intimate. Davenant then knew Hobbes, who knew
Bacon, who knew Ben Jonson, who
was intimate with Beaumont and
Fletcher, Chapman, Donne, Drayton,
Camden, Seldon, Clarendon, Sidney,
Raleigh, and perhaps all the great
men of Elizabeth's and James's time,
the greatest of them all undoubtedly.
Thus have we a link of 'beamy

17—2

hands' from our own times up to Shakespeare.

"In this friendly genealogy we have omitted the numerous side-branches or common friendships. It may be mentioned, however, in order not to omit Spenser, that Davenant resided some time in the family of Lord Brooke, the friend of Sir Phillip Sidney. Spenser's intimacy with Sidney is mentioned by himself in a letter, still extant, to Gabriel Harvey."

XIV.

BY THE RIVER-SIDE.

" It is nothing strange that men who throw their flies for trout should dream of it."—W. C. PRIME.

WHO would not have gone a-fishing with dear old Izaak Walton and his friends, and been one in the quaint and pleasing conversations which took place between them! But as that has been denied us, we can still be with them in spirit as they whip the streams and talk.

" VENATOR. On my word, master, this is a gallant trout. What shall we do with him?

" PISCATOR. Marry, e'en eat him to supper. We'll go to my hostess,

from whence we came. She told me
as I was going out of door that my
brother Peter, a good angler and a
cheerful companion, had sent word
he would lodge there to-night, and
bring a friend with him. My hostess
has two beds, and I know you and I
may have the best. We'll rejoice
with my brother Peter and his friend,
tell tales, or sing ballads, or make a
catch, or find some harmless sport to
content us, and pass away a little
time without offence to either God
or man.

" VENATOR. A match, good master.
Let's go to that house, for the linen
looks white, and smells of lavender,
and I long to lie in a pair of sheets
that smell so. Let's be going, good
master, for I am hungry again with
fishing."

Before they return, however, Piscator catches another logger-headed
chub, which he hangs on a willow

twig, and then indulges in the following observations, which are remarkable for their charming simplicity,
and (to use Sir Walter Scott's expression) for their "Arcadian language" : "Let's be going. But turn
out of the way a little, good scholar,
towards yonder high hedge. We'll
sit whilst this shower falls so gently
upon the teeming earth, and gives a
sweeter smell to the lovely flowers
that adorn the verdant meadows.
Look! under that broad beech-tree,
I sat down when I was last this way
a-fishing, and the birds in the adjoin-
ing grove seemed to have a friendly
contention with an echo, whose dead
voice seemed to live in a hollow cave
near to the brow of that primrose-
hill : there I sat viewing the silver
streams glide silently towards their
centre, the tempestuous sea; yet
sometimes opposed by rugged roots,
and pebble-stones, which broke their

waves, and turned them into foam ; and sometimes viewing the harmless lambs, some leaping securely in the cool shade, whilst others sported themselves in the cheerful sun ; and others were craving comfort from the swollen udders of their bleating dams. As I thus sat, these and other sights had so fully possessed my soul that I thought, as the poet has happily expressed it,

" ' I was for that time lifted above earth ;
  And possest joys not promis'd in my birth.'

"As I left this place and entered into the next field, a second pleasure entertained me. 'Twas a handsome milkmaid, that had cast away all care, and sung like a nightingale. Her voice was good, and the ditty fitted for it. 'Twas that smooth song that was made by Kit Marlowe, now at least fifty years ago, and the milk-maid's mother sung an answer to it, which was made by Sir Walter Raleigh

in his younger days. They were old-
fashioned poetry, but choicely good.
I think much better than that now
in fashion in this critical age. Look
yonder, on my word, yonder they be
a-milking again. I will give her the
chub, and persuade them to sing
those two songs for us."

This dialogue then takes place
between ·Piscator and the milkwoman :

" PISCATOR. God speed, good
woman! I have been a-fishing, and
am going to Bleak Hall to my bed ;
and having caught more fish than
will sup myself and friend, will bestow
this upon you and your daughter, for
I use to sell none.

" MILKWOMAN. Marry, God requite
you, sir! and we'll eat it cheerfully;
and if you come this way a-fishing
two months hence, a grace of God
I'll give you a sillabub of new verjuice
in a new-made haycock, and my

Maudlin shall sing you one of her best ballads, for she and I both love all anglers, they be such honest, civil, quiet men. In the meantime, will you drink a draught of red cow's milk. You shall have it freely?

" PISCATOR. No, I thank you ; but I pray do us a courtesy that shall stand you and your daughter in nothing, and we will think ourselves still something in your debt; it is but to sing us a song, that was sung by you and your daughter when I last passed over this meadow, about eight or nine days since.

" MILKWOMAN. What song was it, I pray ? Was it 'Come, shepherds, deck your heads,' or 'As at noon Dulcina rested,' or 'Philida flouts me'?

" PISCATOR. No, it is none of these; it is a song that your daughter sung the first part, and you sung the answer to it.

" MILKWOMAN. Oh, I know it now! I learned the first part in my golden age, when I was about the age of my daughter; and the latter part, which indeed fits me best, but two or three years ago, when the cares of the world began to take hold of me; but you shall, God willing, hear them both. Come, Maudlin, sing the first part to the gentlemen with a merry heart, and I'll sing the second when you have done."

And so the milkmaid sings, and is answered by a song from her mother. Piscator thanks them, but Venator appears to have expressed his gratitude in a more affectionate manner than his sedate companion approved of, for his master observes: "Scholar, let Maudlin alone; do not offer to spoil her voice. Look, yonder comes my hostess to call us to supper. How, now? Is my brother Peter come?"

" HOSTESS. Yes; and a friend with him. They are both glad to hear you are in these parts, and long to see you; and are hungry, and long to be at supper."

Piscator and Venator then meet "brother Peter," who introduces them to Coridon, "an honest countryman, a most downright, witty, merry companion, that met me here purposely to eat a trout, and to be pleasant."

They sup of the trout which Piscator had caught, with such other meat as the house afforded, moistening their cheer with "some of the best barley wine, the good liquor that our good, honest forefathers did use to drink of, which preserved their health, and made them live so long, and to do so many good deeds."

They then agree to sing several songs and catches, which Venator says "shall give some addition of

mirth to the company, for we will be
merry;" upon which Piscator observes, "'Tis a match, my masters;
let's even say grace, and turn to the
fire, drink the other cup to wet our
whistles, and so sing away all sad
thoughts. Come on, my masters;
who begins? I think it's best to
draw cuts, and avoid contention."
The lot accordingly falls to Coridon,
who begins, for " he hates contention." The song is much admired by
Piscator, who exclaims, " Well sung,
Coridon; this song was sung with
mettle, and was choicely fitted to
the occasion; I shall love you for it
as long as I know you. I would you
were a brother of the angle; for a
companion that is cheerful, and free
from swearing and scurrilous discourse, is worth gold. I love such
mirth as does not make friends
ashamed to look upon one another
next morning ; nor men (that cannot

well bear it) to repent the money
they spend when they be warmed
with drink. And take this for a rule,
you may pick out such times and
such companies that you may make
yourselves merrier for a little than
a great deal of money; for 'tis the
company and not the charge makes
the feast. And such a companion
you prove; I thank you for it. But
I will not compliment you out of the
debt that I owe you, and, therefore,
I will begin my song, and wish it
may be as well liked."

Piscator is also rewarded for his
song by the applause of his companions: and, after the following
dialogue, they separate for the night:

"CORIDON. Well sung, brother!
you have paid your debt in good
coin. We anglers are all beholden
to the good man that made this song.
Come, hostess, give us more ale, and
let's drink to him. And now let's

everyone go to bed, that we may rise early; but first let's pay our reckoning, for I will have nothing to hinder me in the morning, for my purpose is to prevent the sun-rising.

"PETER. A match! I know, brother, you and your scholar will lie together; but where shall we meet to-morrow night? for my friend Coridon and I will go up the water towards Ware.

"PISCATOR. And my scholar and I will go down towards Waltham.

"CORIDON. Then let's meet here, for here are fresh sheets that smell of lavender; and I am sure that we cannot expect better meat, or better usage, in any place.

"PETER. 'Tis a match. Good-night to everybody!"

Elliot Stock, 62, Paternoster Row, London.

www.ingramcontent.com/pod-product-compliance
Lightning Source LLC
Chambersburg PA
CBHW020811060726
47498CB00017B/1622